T0199110

DIABOLIC SOUNDS
of
SILICON VALLEY

C. REA JORDAN

DIABOLIC SOUNDS OF SILICON VALLEY

iUniverse books may be ordered through booksellers or by contacting:

iUniverse
1663 Liberty Drive
Bloomington, IN 47403
www.iuniverse.com
1-800-Authors (1-800-288-4677)

ISBN: 978-1-5320-6058-8 (sc)
ISBN: 978-1-5320-6057-1 (e)

Print information available on the last page.

iUniverse rev. date: 10/19/2018

CONTENTS

CHAPTER 1

HOSTILE TAKEOVER RUMORS

The drive to the office took about 20 minutes, and he was parking in the Executives Parking Section, Spot #3 marked "VICE PRESIDENT". He liked his executive privileges, the reserved parking spot marked with the Vice President title. He looked at the vacant parking spot #2, Executive Vice President, and smiled. As he walked past spot #1 stenciled "President", he stopped and glanced at the three-story office building that was Biotherm. He mumbled, "Carlton Herrick named President" and whispered "piece of cake". He liked his private office with the thick, wall to wall, slate gray carpet. As he entered the building, he was greeted by the security guard with a two-finger salute, a wink, and a nod. Carlton reached into his inside coat pocket to show his ID badge, but the guard held up his hand, palm forward and he winked again, "Good morning, Mr. Herrick. Not necessary, Mr. Herrick. How 'bout this rain?"

"Feels kinda' nice, Jessie. Makes the wheat grow, huh?

The guard nodded his head like a chicken pecking corn. "Here in California its rice, Mr. Herrick."

Once inside walking through the maze of cubicles, Carlton slowed as he neared the cubicle occupied by Julie Vissetti. Her eyes darted both directions before she puckered her lips into a symbolic kiss and returned her attention to the monitor screen on her desk.

He stood in front of his office door admiring the brass nameplate. He turned checking both directions before he leaned forward, blew his warm breath on the nameplate and gave it a quick wipe with the sleeve of his raincoat. The carpet felt thick and luxuriant under his Italian Ferragamo shoes. It felt like walking on clouds. Without removing his raincoat, he went directly to his desk and placed his briefcase on the desk. He opened the calendar on his cell phone placing it near the intercom device. Comfortably seated in his Corinthian leather chair, he unfolded the Examiner article, leaned back and read the article again for the third or fourth time.

The Examiner article has reported deaths from exotic diseases around the world. Toxins and deadly poisons are studied by scientists led by Harmon Azran, M.D., Ph.D. at the Azran Clinic for exotic disease.

Carlton took the folded note from his raincoat pocket and reviewed the history of the UPS deliveries to Azran's clinic. Satisfied that all elements were in place, he put the UPS data and the Examiner article back into his briefcase and put the briefcase in the bottom, locked drawer of his desk.

The phone rang. He answered on the first ring.

"Yes, Carlton Herrick here."

"Mr. Herrick, This is Juliette. You had four early calls this morning and your wife called around nine. You have a departmental meeting scheduled for 11 AM this morning. May I come in, and go over your schedule?"

"Good morning, Juliette. Yes, of course. Please, get me a phone number for the Azran Clinic in Menlo Park?"

He walked to the coat closet and as he was hanging up his coat, Juliette walked into the room closing the door behind her. The phone's insistent ringing interrupted his thoughts.

Juliette answered the phone on his desk.

"Good morning, this is Juliette, Mr. Herrick's secretary. How may ----- Yes, sir, yes, sir, he is in the office. Yes, sir, I'll tell him you want him in your office right away".

"Okay, Julie, brief me on today's activities.

Juliette interrupted. "He wants you in his office now."

"Yes", Carlton replied. "But first I want to hear what rumors you hear around the office?"

"That was Mr. Bondurant, Carlton. He sounds really aggravated about something.

Carlton smiled with his mouth and frowned with his eyes. "We can talk later, okay?" She closed both eyes and smiled at him. Carlton was aware of her more than casual interest. However, he was against office fraternization.

As Carlton walked into Alex Bondurant's office, he straightened his tie, cleared his throat and took a deep breath through his nose. His chest swelled as he spoke, "Good morning, Alex. How are you, sir?"

"Skip the social graces, Carlton, and sit down. It is vital that we draw up a battle plan or we may both be saying 'bye bye' to our executive comforts, our perquisites and maybe our 401(k) as well."

"At your service, general," Carlton joked as he sat down. "I thought the joint venture with Gigatrax Ltd. was moving smoothly. What's going on?"

"Carlton, I didn't give you the whole picture last month. It is not just a simple joint venture. It may be, an acquisition attempt --- more than that, it might be a hostile takeover. I'm sorry I couldn't tell you more then."

"Well, Alex, the situation is not dire, right? Just a mite more complicated. We still maintain control and the Board names you as Chair of the combined operation, right?"

"No, Carlton. Clarence Harwood --- you know Clarence --- on our Board. Well, Clarence holds significant equity in Biotherm. He has a strong vote on our Board and is not without considerable influence."

"Yes, I know, but Clarence has high regard for you, and I know when I was promoted, Clarence supported your recommendation. I don't see a problem. Besides that, if his shares are not fully vested, some significant equity can be back on our table."

"Your point is valid and well taken, C. R. but if we were blindsided. You know Max Becker over at Gigatrax?"

"I do, of course, but I'm not all that impressed with him."

"Suggest you get more impressed with Max Becker. Get to know him, his real strength as well as his weaker areas. His father controls Bellingham Bank and Trust, and provides financial support to Gigatrax."

"I will do just that as you are suggesting. I accept the challenge."

"--- and he keeps Max firmly entrenched as Pres. and CEO. Several months ago, office rumors circulated that our Board was planning to make a motion in executive session and you were excluded from that private meeting. The motion was to bring Max Becker here into Biotherm as Exec VP."

"Hell, Alex. When did you start listening to rumors?"

"Not a rumor, Carlton. Max's Mother's sister is married to Clarence Harwood.

"Whoa, just a minute, Alex. You lost me."

"Okay, Max's Mother has a Sister who happens to be Clarence Harwood's wife."

"So, Clarence is on our board and he is Max's Uncle. Give me the bottom line, Alex."

"Close, but not quite, Carlton. Clarence is Max's Brother-in-Law."

"Too much for me to comprehend. Ancestry to me is about the same as integral calculus, Alex."

"I understand. It does get complicated and Clarence's equity position is a constant threat to me, to you and to Biotherm.."

"You are joking, I gotta' ask. How or why is he still on our board, Alex?"

Alex reached into his desk for his little bottle of nitroglycerin pills, "That is the question, Carlton. You can see why the anxiety is aggravating me. Understand, if you will, Clarence is supporting the re-organization, he leans toward voting to name Max as Exec VP and Chief Operating Officer of the merged organization."

"You as Chairman and CEO, right?"

"Wrong. I get the option to resign or move to Amsterdam as Sr. VP of European Operations. That's scuttlebutt. Nevertheless, it is not too difficult to clearly see Max in full command as President and CEO with you and me pushed out."

"Damn it, Alex. I am seeing the picture now with Clarence stepping in as Exec. V.P. or even C.O.E., right? We can't let this happen."

"Hold on a minute, C. R. --- It gets worse. Whether it comes down as a hostile takeover or a nice cooperative venture, maybe even, a romance merger, Gigatrax Ltd. will be the surviving organization. If push comes to hostile takeover, you get the proverbial goodbye kiss with no gold watch."

"Alex, it is way too early in the year for April Fool jokes. You are talking about my career going down the toilet. How are you positioning? At the risk of affronting your sensibilities, Alex, or your comfort with the Ten Commandments, there are ways to clear the road ahead. I suggest that aggression is the strongest defense."

"Whoa there, Carlton. I am not going to ask you to expound on any clandestine ideas you may be conjuring up."

"I know, Alex. Yet, there is a way to get from one point to another that is not a straight line."

"It won't matter, Carlton. I've always backed you and will continue to do so, but the Chair and the Presidency will not be offered to me, and that is no joke either. I'm with our corporate legal team this afternoon and need to take care of a few other details. I want you to meet with me and legal counsel at dinner this evening. Maurice's at seven. Okay?"

Carlton walked out and headed back to his office.

Juliette was waiting in Carlton's office pouring coffee for him as he walked through the door. She spoke without turning around.

"The Azran Clinic number and info is on your desk, Carlton, with a fresh cup of coffee. I ground the beans and made it fresh just like you like it."

Balancing the cup, on one hand, she walked over to the door activating the privacy lock. She placed the porcelain cup of steaming coffee on the tray in front of Carlton and sat down crossing her legs provocatively. The side split in her skirt accentuated long, smoothly muscled, sun-bronzed legs that could have been used in any TV ad for suntan lotion, expensive shoes or beach wear. Julie was sensuously shaped and might have been a million dollar model for abbreviated swimming wear. Carlton sipped his dark, Columbian brew.

"Relax and enjoy the coffee, Carlton", she said.

"I can't relax, Julie. Alex just confirmed my suspicions about the merger talks going on between Biotherm and Gigatrax, and it is worse than I expected. I thought I had the Exec VP spot guaranteed, nailed down, signed and delivered --- almost. Now, it is all looking topsy-turvey."

"It will work out, Carlton", she assured him. She leaned forward, unbuttoned the top of her blouse with the deliberate intent to improve Carlton's obvious consternation.

Carlton showed no apparent physiological interest. Julie always interested Carlton in more of a professionally platonic way.

"Julie. What is the talk out on the floor?"

"Carlton, I'm not supposed to know anything and definitely not talk about anything. The people on the floor know nothing about any joint venture --- not even rumors."

"That's good. What have you heard from Marcella Winslow, Alex's private spy? She never briefs me."

"Well, Ms. Winslow says that Max Becker is related to one of our board members."

"I know that already. What else did she say?"

"No, you don't know this already. She said that Gigatrax Ltd. will probably be the surviving company, and Max Becker will get the Board's support to take over as President. She said your boss, Mr. Bondurant, had planned on moving you up to Exec. V.P., but the Board plans to meet in private, executive session to discuss that pending decision."

Julie's omnipresent happy attitude and bright smile faded and the corners of her mouth turned downward hiding her perfect white teeth. Carlton was keenly aware of facial expressions, body positions and movements. It was only a minor, insignificant study of Juliette's eyes beginning to tear up as she dabbed at tears emerging from her eyes that Carlton patted her hand. As she sniffed and cleared her throat trying to escape the choked up feeling that was overtaking her, she whispered, "If you ever leave here, Carlton. I will never stay here and work for Max Becker."

"Julie, re-schedule the 11 A.M. meeting. I'll be out of the office. You can reach me on the cell phone if you hear anything else. I'll be out until this afternoon --- sometime after 2:30. I'll be with Alex and the corporate legal beagles tonight at Maurice's. I'll call you after the dinner meeting.

CHAPTER 2

PLANNING THE THEFT

Carlton's strategy was simple as most any other business decision. He had considered the problem analytically. The same management talent applied. Define the objective, develop a strategy and initiate action. A systematic plan was his trademark. He could kill Max Becker if necessary and Carlton was sure as hell going to be ready.

The sky was a dismal gray blur and the intermittent rain was the threat of a depressing day. Carlton Herrick paced up and down the short block across the street from the loading and receiving dock of the Azran Clinic for Febrile and Exotic Disease as he had been doing for the past several weeks. He turned up the collar of his raincoat against the wind and cold raindrops hit his cheek. Walking in either direction, he could keep the loading dock easily in view. Yesterday morning, the UPS delivery van had arrived at 8:10. The day before that the UPS deliveries were closer to 8:30, and three days ago, the truck showed up at exactly 8:20. Carlton Herrick pushed his shirt sleeve back from his right wrist and glanced at his watch and checked the time. It was 8:23. He reached the corner, turned to retrace his path, glanced across the street as the brown UPS truck pulled into the hospital's loading dock. Max checked his watch again before taking a notepad from his coat pocket, and wrote "Thurs., Oct. 7th 8:26". He closed the notepad and tucked it into the pocket of his raincoat.

Carton Herrick was conscious of his image. He wore expensive things like custom-made shirts and expensive, Italian suits. Women always gave him a second look, but his smile often came close to a sneer and did serve to fend off comments or criticisms regarding some of his more questionable behavior.

Carlton started with Biotherm as a salesman and his aggressive tactics and absolute lack of ethics earned him the District Sales Manager spot after only two years. It took another two years to move up to Regional Sales Manager. Two months into his new R.M. responsibility, the National Sales Manager was incapacitated in a skiing accident. Carlton got the job. He was in Palo Alto within two weeks, bought a nice home in Los Altos Hills and set his sights on the next rung up the corporate ladder. Carlton was an expert at developing strong relationships with executives already up the corporate food chain. His sales records over the last four years had gained him the attention of the board of directors and a strong ally and personal friend in his boss, the company president, Alex Bondurant. The Board had unanimously approved his Vice Presidency last quarter. The mention of the name, Carlton Herrick, was synonymous with the golden boy. A few of his peers had other less glamorous monikers for Carlton's in-fighting abilities.

Rumors around the industry suggested that Gigatrax, Max Becker's company, was a hungry giant planning to buy up controlling shares of Biotherm with the threat of takeover. Carlton Herrick knew his executive position would be under heavy fire, and his career seriously threatened. His business ethics and behavior were aggressive, vicious and instances of savagery could be remembered by past competitors in business or, for that matter, racquetball. He had decided to take any action necessary to take Max Becker out of the competition.

Carlton's philosophy as he liked to say was, 'It is not how you play the game as long as you win'. He began spending lots of time researching unusual circumstances of death. He fantasized about Max Becker choking to death at dinner. He found articles about the likelihood of choking on various types of food, and he noted that hot dogs ranked very high. This was quickly abandoned because he could not induce the choking. He became an amateur expert on dangerous mushrooms. Neurotoxins, poisons that attacked the nervous system, captured his attention. Eating poisonous fish in a Japanese restaurant was intriguing to Carlton. He learned that the fish that the Japanese call Fugu contains a neurotoxin that will paralyze a person and induce death by suffocation, but he was not able to find any restaurants or sources for such a dangerous delicacy. Weeks before, he had found an article in the San Francisco Examiner about some new treatment for immune deficiency disorders, and Dr. Harman Azran was described as a modern-day medical miracle worker. Carlton had developed an almost morbid interest in epidemiology. Tropical and febrile disease fascinated him, and he absorbed anything he could find relating to that topic. The newspaper described promising research work being done at Dr. Azran's Clinic for Febrile and

Exotic Disease which was near Palo Alto in Menlo Park. Carlton had cut the article out of the paper and filed it in his briefcase.

Over the past weeks, Carlton had made these repeated trips to the Azran Clinic and made notes of entrances, exits, traffic, patient parking, doctor parking, emergency vehicle ingress, and egress. The methods in his plan required him to locate Dr. Azran's office, determine Azran's hours at the clinic, the location of the doctors' lounge and the precise time of daily UPS deliveries to the clinic. He had made drawings of the exits and entrances to the building and schedules of traffic, employees comings and goings and patient flow.

His activity plan for today had been met. He mentally applauded himself for completing every objective he had planned for today. Within the next day or so, he would go into the Clinic right after the UPS deliveries were made and locate Azran's office and the Doctor's lounge. The task tomorrow might take ten minutes but could take longer depending on how quickly he might find one of Dr. Azran's business cards and a lab coat with Azran's name embroidered on it.

Carlton mentally reviewed his entire plan in detail as he continued walking and observing every activity around the Azran Clinic. He considered the possibilities of being caught or discovered within the Clinic. He had minimal concern about interrupting a UPS delivery and getting a package intended for Dr. Azran. However, he resolved this small concern deciding he would solve each and every problem if and when it happened.

CHAPTER 3

AZRAN CLINIC FOR
EXOTIC DISEASE

The cold, early winter wind blew through the oak trees and scattered dead leaves around the grounds of the Azran Clinic. The two-story building combined a medical research facility with the clinic and an impressive, three-hundred, bed hospital. Inside, as a result of grants and stipends from the National Institutes of Health, and Angel investors. Medical devices filled every room. A bibliography of technical publications on most exotic or febrile disease would list Dr. Azran's name in, at least, a thousand learned publications.

Two young scientists, highly sophisticated physicians/surgeons are expert for a variety of ailments and disorders.

Dr. Corbin Neeley, a gastroenterologist, and electromagnetic specialist is the youngest staff member at Azran Clinic. Dr. Neeley using grants and private investments allocates a significant percentage of his hours at the clinic developing electromagnetic devices with potential for clinical, surgical or diagnostic applications. With degrees and experience in veterinary medicine, he continues certain areas of his veterinary interests. His social graces were lost or discarded early before his professional education. His intense focus and concentration on resolving medical ailments cause him to be abrupt and short tempered. At times, especially with female patients, he is affable and an effective communicator. Corbin is tall, handsome and physically attractive with a chiseled profile, thick, brown hair, and a winning smile. With otherwise favorable characteristics, Corbin is not the nice guy; he is more aptly described as unfriendly.

Corbin's undergraduate degree was a BSEE with honors in electronic engineering. Much of his earlier research work with domestic animals involved high technology electromagnetic devices which he felt had extraordinary, reparative capability for skeletal/muscular malfunctions or disorders.

The other scientist working under Dr. Harman Azran is Gunter Hertzmann. Gunter, a tall, blue-eyed, blonde-haired German from Stuttgart Germany who was attracted to the Azran Clinic upon his graduation from Heidelberg Medical College. Gunter Hertzmann, M.D., Ph.D. was trained in exotic diseases which was the credential that earned his position with Dr. Azran. He has a natural, military bearing which may be one cause of the periodic friction between him and Dr. Neeley.

Garbed in surgical scrubs, Dr. Neeley is standing under the bright, surgical lights of the operating room performing a surgical procedure on an anesthetized dog.

The alarm on the surgical room door sounded as Gunter noisily entered.

"Damn, Corbin! Smells like hell in here." Gunter Hertzmann interrupted the intensity of Dr. Neeley's work.

"It did not smell until you came in, Gunter. Come here, Gunter. I'll explain and I need your help for a minute or so."

"What do you want, Corbin. Maybe, if you ask nicely."

"Gunter! Gimme' a hand here, will you? Corbin motioned in the air with his gloved hand. "Over there on the instrument bench. Adjust the Megger voltage to 150 millivolts while I observe this animal's response."

"Will do, Corbin. One twenty, one fifty --- mv! Done! Now, Corbin, tell me what we are doing here to this animal." Gunter observed the paroxysmal spasms of the anesthetized animal.

Corbin adjusted a micro Wheatstone bridge attached to a magnetic coil of wire implanted in the dog's urinary tract as he explained, "This electromagnet, Gunter, allows me to subtly train the ureter and we are blue toothing 150 millivolts to the --- ."

"Well," interjected Gunter, "and what is the objective?"

"This Labrador Retriever has an incontinence behavioral problem. The electrical field that we are applying now will encourage stem cell migration. Corbin hesitated. "--- and teach him to stop pissing in the house."

Gunter placed his big hand on Corbin's shoulder. "Whatever, good to see that you are not dabbling with a gadget to solve some bacterial infection."

Corbin responded in an irritated manner, "Even bacterial infections can be ameliorated with electromagnetic devices --- verstehen, Gunter?"

"Nevertheless, Corbin, disease management is not as simple as turning a switch on or off."

"True, Gunter. However, it should be that simple and it is within the realm of possibility."

The intercom beeped. Gunter and Corbin heard Verna Kellar's voice. "Dr. Neeley, I need to speak to you when you are available."

Gunter wagged his index finger as he shook his head left and right and sneered at Corbin.

Corbin growled, "Gunter, heraus! Got it? Get out of my lab --- now!

"Your German is worse than your magnetic junk. Du bist ein Dummkopf!" Gunter walked around a lab bench in order to kick over a waste can as he left.

"Oh gosh, Gunter, I forgot you are licensed to butcher the English language, right?"

Corbin called Verna's extension. "You want to talk to me, Verna?"

"Later maybe, Corbin. Right now I am going on break and making a run over to the grocery store to pick up a few, personal things. Do you want me to bring anything back for you?"

"Just a soft drink of some kind, maybe. That is all. Well, no, I'd like a Blood Orange juice or if you can't find it, a Root Beer. We can talk when you return."

"Corbin, I have never even heard of any drink called Blood Orange and who would ever drink it if it really existed --- anyway. There are plenty of cold drinks in the kitchen."

"Never mind, Verna. If it is too much bother for you, Corbin teased, "just bring me back a carton of Buttermilk."

"Are you serious, doctor Neeley, Verna smirked, "do you actually drink Buttermilk?"

"Don't ask, Verna, just go. ---Okay?"

"Yes, okay, but if I come back with your buttermilk, you better drink all of it."

"Okay, Verna, look for Bulgarian Cultured buttermilk which is an excellent probiotic containing several active organisms --- ah, you know, Lactobacillus vulgaris ---"

"Corbin, I did not go to med school. What are probiotics anyway?

"I'll teach you things like this later, Verna."

CHAPTER 4

SOUNDS OF PAIN

A s Verna entered the grocery store, she had expected the temperature in the store to be warmer than the weather outside. The store's air conditioning seemed louder than usual. She rushed through the store adding a jar of pickles, a box of tissues, a roll of breath mints, Spearmint chewing gum and lastly a bottle of olive oil to her cart. She had a vague feeling that she was forgetting something. She laughed thinking about Corbin's asking for buttermilk. She backtracked into the store and added a bottle of orange soda pop to her cart.

After paying, the cashier handed her change and a clerk packaged her items in a brown, paper bag. The clerk asked, "May I help you with your bag?"

Verna saw the clerk's mouth moving but heard not a single word.

The sound was an explosive crescendo. It started with a discomforting rumble but grew immediately to sounds like bomb explosions. Verna Kellar dropped her grocery bag and opened her mouth screaming as she fell to the floor. She clamped her hands over her ears to shield against the pain. She bit down on the inside of her lower lip until a trickle of blood oozed from her mouth. The pitch of the sound vibrated until the decibel level drove pain from her eardrums to her teeth and eyes. After agonizing moments, the grating cacophony softened to the usual sounds of the grocery store. Verna wiped her eyes, started picking up groceries and cut her finger on the glass from the broken pickle jar. Tears formed in both eyes as she clenched her fists trying to stop her trembling hands.

A small crowd of people formed a circle around Verna and began picking up the spilled groceries. A young man with a roll of paper towels was soaking up pickle juice, olive oil, and orange soda pop. Verna stared at the colored mixture on the floor mentally comparing it to an ugly abstract painting. A feeling of aggravation about her absurd illusion brought back her sense of reality.

"Pardon me miss but are you okay?" The young man extended his hand offering a paper towel. I can call an ambulance for you."

Verna glanced at the paper towel turning the offer down with a slight shake of her head. "The noise," she said, "was awful."

"Here is a clean handkerchief. Your nose is bleeding. Take this." He handed her the clean hanky.

She took it and dabbed at her nose. "What was that noise?"

"What noise? I didn't hear anything." He focused on a small blood spot on her thin, silk blouse just above her erect nipple. He smiled as he stared at the outline of her breasts. His smile lasciviously showed years of dental neglect.

"That noise!" She waved her hand in a circular motion over her head. A tear eased down her cheek. She blotted it with the inside of her wrist.

Using his pinkie finger, he tapped at the corner of his mouth. "You have a little bit of blood right here."

"You didn't hear that rumbling noise? I thought the building was collapsing," she questioned as she held the corner of the handkerchief to her mouth.

"I'm fine. I can't believe you didn't hear that noise." Verna leaned away avoiding his acute halitosis which was much too bad to be called bad breath. Her facial expression indicated the violation of her sense of cleanliness.

"How 'bout a cup of coffee. I'll get you a Band-Aid. Our bakery department has the best coffee in Walnut Creek, maybe in California."

"Gotta' go, but thanks for the offer and for your concern. I'm okay."

She turned and started to walk away as she responded. "I work at Azran Clinic over on Hospital Drive and should have been back thirty minutes ago."

"I'm Coby Ryan, the store manager here. Would you like someone to drive you back to work?"

"No, thanks, I think I could use the walk."

"And, if you want a clerk to bag the products that fell and broke. No charge, of course."

"What? No, never mind. No, it isn't important now. Thanks. Bye."

As Verna approached the automatic exit door, she noticed a well-dressed man walking toward her. He smiled conveying his friendly manner and spoke, "Excuse me, Miss, you probably did not notice but I was one of the people helping you pick up your groceries. I'd guess that mishap was not in your plans for today."

Verna flashed one of her most innocent poses and responded, "Well, I think it might best be called awkward stupidity more than a mishap."

"I overheard you pass up a ride from someone in the store. My car is right there parked at the curb. You have earned a comfortable ride back to work. I'm Carlton Herrick and driving right past --- you said Azran Clinic, didn't you?"

"Yes, Mr. Herrick, on second thought, I'll take your offer and thanks for helping me during my embarrassing moments in the store. Yes, my name is Verna Kellar. I do work at Azran Clinic.

"Friends call me Carlton, Verna. I have read about the Clinic and Dr. Azran's scientific contributions to medicine. I think meeting him would be an enjoyable experience."

"If you are genuinely interested in meeting doctor Azran, I can make an appointment next week if you like. Oh! There is the clinic ahead on the right."

"Verna, if I call the clinic, will I reach you?"

"Do you live here, Carlton?"

"No, Verna, I live in the Bay Area but I know Walnut Creek pretty well."

"How did you happen to shop where you observed me fall and drop all my groceries?"

"Oh! My sister and her family live in Walnut Creek."

"So, meeting in the store was pure happenstance?"

"Well, Verna, I'd prefer to call it just fortunate circumstances."

"Of course, I'm the full-time receptionist here and thanks for the ride and your earlier consideration."

Verna walked up the ramp toward the employees' entrance thinking what a good-looking guy she had just met.

Opening the entry door, she stopped with a disgusted puff of air, remembering Dr. Neeley's orange soda pop.

CHAPTER 5

FDA INSPECTOR INTRUSION

Corbin Neeley's office was spacious and a shade under opulent with thick carpets surrounded by natural granite tiles and a water feature with the relaxing sounds of a bubbling brook. Corbin was relaxing at his desk with a cup of coffee as he scanned the Journal of Gastroenterology. After the fourth ring, he answered, "Yes, this is Dr. Neeley."

"Dr. Neeley, this is Armand Covari. I'm the compliance inspector for the FDA, the Food and Drug Administration."

"It is not necessary to explain who or what the FDA is or does," Dr. Neeley growled like an attack dog. "How did you get my private number?"

"Listen, Doctor, I'm up front here in the reception area of your office. I need just a few minutes of your time to discuss your registration as a medical device manufacturer---"

Dr. Neeley interrupted. "Excuse me, Mr. Covari. I don't have the time to read to you from the Federal Register. Were you competent in your job, you would already know that I am a veterinarian as well as a medical gastroenterologist ---"

The FDA inspector took his turn at interrupting. "Doctor, you are manufacturing a medical device. However, you are not registered as a Medical Device Manufacturer, and you have not filed a 510(k) with the FDA --- and ---"

"Shut up and listen and I'll take the time to explain what you should have been taught by your superiors. Now! Shut up and listen to me. The FDA as published in the Federal Register classified two categories --- namely drugs and devices. More importantly, young man, and listen carefully; devices are not regulated by the FDA in veterinary applications."

"Sir! --- ah, Dr. Neeley ---" The voice of exasperation was loud and clear. "I have no more time or patience with your apparent ignorance or impudence. This telephone conversation is at a conclusion." Corbin Neeley slammed his fist onto the membrane switch attempting to close the communication system.

Corbin still was hammering on the membrane switch when Covari barged through Corbin's office door.

Jumping from his chair, Corbin screamed. "Get the hell out of here, you simple shit."

"Two minutes, doctor --- just two minutes is all the time I need." Armand held his hands palm to palm under his chin in supplication. His manner and apparent attitude had morphed him into a pitiful beggar.

Corbin lunged at Covari and held up his fist in a threatening gesture. "Damn you! You simple-minded piece of worthless crap. Obviously, you have no understanding of the off-label use of devices or drugs that lack FDA sanctions but which the doctor deems in the best interest of an ailing patient."

Corbin's lunge grew to a two-handed shove.

Covari stumbled backward and fell to the floor. Corbin hesitated and observed Covari struggling to stand. Once erect on his feet, he raked his arm across Corbin's desk spreading papers and reports all over the floor. Covari stuttered and stammered with vicious intent to keep Corbin from approaching him.

"You, bastard, Neeley, are nobody other than a totally arrogant ass. I will generate a scathing, non-compliance report to Silver Springs with details of your brutal attack on me. Expect to be contacted by FDA Compliance Officers. I will leave here and go to the police department to file against you. My attorney will be instructed to file against you for malpractice."

Covari spun around facing the door; Corbin grabbed Covari's briefcase out of his hand throwing it to the floor.

Covari turned to face Corbin mumbling. "I have powerful friends. I could get your license pulled with a phone call. You jackass." Mucus from Armand Covari's nose dripped to the floor as he cursed and left the room.

"Get outta' here --- you village idiot!"

Corbin was gasping for breath. His face became a deep crimson shade of red. His hands trembled as he poured water from a desk decanter into a paper cup, and fumbled through his desk searching for his pills to bring his blood pressure back under control. He found a capsule and reached for the cup of water. His agitation and trembling hands resulted in spilling the water over all the papers already on the floor. He swallowed the capsule dry mumbling,

"What the hell was his name?" He boldly printed A-r-m-a-n -d C-o-v-a-r-i on a scrap of paper and immediately crushed it throwing it on the floor.

The intercom light flashed green indicating that the call was coming from inside the building. Corbin glanced at the Caller ID screen before reacting. "Hey, Verna. I didn't forget you. Why don't you come on in and let's talk, but first, give me ten minutes to cool down until I feel normal again."

"Alright, but should I just wait for you in the exam room. I had another incident at the grocery store this morning." Verna began to tear up and wiped her cheek with the back of her hand. "Am I going nuts, Dr. Neeley?"

"No self-diagnosis, Verna. Sure --- just come on into my office?"

Corbin stood up as Verna came in; he motioned for her to sit down next to the water feature. Verna Kellar had been hired as a receptionist five years ago when she was twenty- two years old. Now at twenty-seven, she had matured into a sexually attractive, long-legged woman with perfectly formed breasts; nipples that erected at the slightest breeze or an admiring glance. As she relaxed into the chair, Corbin patted her knee. "Now just listen to that water serenade for a few seconds. That should make you feel much more comfortable. When you feel ready, tell me whatever is on your mind."

She shrugged her shoulders, took a long, slow breath and said, "I'm fine now, but I had a terrible experience this morning. I'm not sure that I can even describe what happened. I had finished shopping and was on my way out of the store when a noise --- no, it was more than a noise --- a sound, very loud vibrating like sound --- and --- like the beginning of an explosion --- like the building was collapsing."

"It is okay Verna, relax and just take it easy for a few minutes. There is a good explanation." Corbin Neeley was adept at patronizing patients. "I can tell you everything but not here in my office."

"Well, Corbin ---"

"Verna, here in the office I am Dr. Neeley, please. Professional image and all."

"Unhuh, I see! We are friends with benefits, but at the office, I'm supposed to treat you like some kind of big shot." Verna pouted and she sniffled a few times.

"Verna, can we not talk about this right now, please." Corbin was still hyper from his earlier episode with the FDA person.

"Alright, it's just that since you did the pelvic exam, I've had stomach cramps and pain right here," she patted the area below her navel.

"Nothing for you to worry about, Verna. The pain you describe is probably no more than a temporary soreness. The anatomical term for the area is the mons veneris, and sometimes if sex becomes overly vigorous, some of the pelvic muscles complain". Corbin's tone took on a slow, soothing, balm-like quality.

"Corbin --- Dr. Neeley, I think it must be more than just soreness. I have seen blood in my urine."

"Uh-huh, easily explained, Verna. You were anesthetized when I did the pelvic exam, I did find a small polyp, and I excised it. Matter of fact, I had it biopsied to be sure it was completely benign."

"Corbin, you told me nothing about taking anything out. You said you just wanted to take a look. Why did you go about this so secretively anyway?"

"Don't worry, Verna, you are fine, perfectly healthy, and I didn't want to burden you with worries about some non-existent problem.

"What about the pain and the bloody discharge?" Consternation brought wrinkles to her face.

"I'll get you some pills to take care of that. Okay? Stop taking aspirin for a few days. It will help."

"At the grocery, I heard noises like heavy equipment, real loud, rumbling noises that seemed to be coming out of my own body, and the pain was horrible." Verna moved her head side to side recalling her anguish at the grocery store.

Corbin looked at his watch, arranged some papers remaining on his desk and glanced back toward Verna.

"Verna, nothing to worry about. The noise could easily have been genuine, and only exaggerated in your mind. Now, don't start going non-compos on me." He patted her on the knee and stood. He turned and nodded, "I'll call you later. I have several hours of work pending in the animal lab."

"I'm not happy with your answers, Corbin. We will discuss this further or I will see some other doctor and --- maybe, explain the entire matter to Dr. Azran."

"You just slow down a notch and get yourself in control. Do not discuss this matter with anyone."

"Dr. Neeley, this whole problem is your fault and I expect you to resolve everything that happened."

"You have my promise. You know that I really care for you. This will be handled perfectly this week."

CHAPTER 6

SCIENTISTS ARGUE

The animal lab was a repository of strange and irritating odors. The chemical section had a characteristic phenol odor. The contiguous animal cages and dog runs were in odoriferous contrast. Cages and runs were sprayed each day with a masking agent.

The animal lab had an elaborate audio system with sound resolution ranging from almost 20 Hertz to nearly 20,000 Hertz. The seemingly absurd range of frequencies was reluctantly approved for the expensive installation. Dr. Azran questioned the need for frequencies that humans are not capable of hearing. However, the music in the animal lab was like sitting in the best seat at the Vienna Music Conservatory.

Gunter Hertzmann crept into the animal lab on tiptoe with a slight wave of his hand. Without any other movement, Corbin lifted his eyebrows from the operating table acknowledging Gunter's presence.

"Wie gehts, Dr. Frankenstein. Let me look over your shoulder. I'm interested in seeing how the Lab is doing," Gunter joked. In the same moment, he saw that the patient was not the dog. "What happened to the Labrador with the pissing problem?"

Corbin shook his head and his face contorted with agitation. "I am in no mood for your humor or your irritating criticism, Gunter."

"Well, Dr. Neeley, you may be trained in veterinary surgery, but experimental surgery on a dog is past borderline. It would seem that you have escalated to primates now. Is that a Rhesus monkey you are about to anesthetize?" Dr. Hertzmann's voice had a scathing edge that caused Dr. Neeley to place the hypodermic syringe back atop the sterile tray, turn and pull down his face mask. "Gunter, it's a fuckin' monkey and it is no concern of yours. Dr. Neeley's voice had an edge sharper than his scalpel.

Dr. Hertzmann decided to avoid the confrontation. "I want to talk to you later today, Corbin. I expect an explanation of your medical involvement with Verna."

"You what! What in hell are you talking about, Gunter? I do not have to justify my professional relationships with you, Gunter. Do I make that clear to you? Corbin had just picked up the syringe. With his outburst, it had fallen to the floor. The glass cartridge broke and a viscous, yellow liquid drained onto the white tile floor.

"Au contraire, my arrogant friend, in this case, you do. If Dr. Azran knew you were running in vivo experimental surgeries with healthy animals, and with no research protocol whatsoever, he would terminate your grant money or terminate you." Gunter's jaw muscles rippled, and his nostrils flared.

"If you are threatening to report my work to Dr. Azran, I suggest you use caution, and it is in your best interest to keep your opinions to yourself. Would you like to have your Visa canceled? I have political friends."

"Corbin, I'm not running to Dr. Azran. Your work in veterinary applications, as you so caustically point out, is your business. However, I do want to have a private and personal talk with you about Verna. Perhaps, we can talk later in a more relaxed way.

"On that matter, Gunter, my relationship with Verna is professional and none of your business."

"Wrong again, Corbin. I'm going to have a meeting with Verna. I want to hear her side, and you can be sure that I will get to the bottom of whatever malfeasance exists." Gunter's jaw tightened and he gritted his teeth making a sound like fingernails scraping across a blackboard. As he left the operating room, he stopped, turned and looked back at Dr. Neeley with an expression of disdain.

Gunter headed toward the clinic's cafeteria as he passed Verna's desk, he stopped waiting for her to finish a telephone call. "Verna, I'm going to get a hot cup of coffee. Will you join me? There are things I'd like to discuss with you."

"Of course, sounds like a good idea especially the cup of hot coffee".

Verna selected a table in the corner of the cafeteria waiting for Gunter to sit down. "May I get your coffee for you Dr. Hertzmann?"

"No, Verna. I'm capable and accustomed to waiting on myself."

They returned to their table after preparing their coffees.

"Okay? What did you want to talk about?"

"Nothing of great consequence. However, I do want to talk in confidence if that is acceptable to you, Verna."

"Dr. Hertzmann, is it something about my work? Have I done something wrong?"

"No, no, not at all Verna. You do an excellent job. I have a question about the dog that was in the animal lab for several weeks."

"The Labrador? Is that the one you are asking about Dr. Hertzmann?"

"Exactly Verna. Do you know what surgeries Dr. Neeley was performing on that dog?"

"Doctor, I am uncomfortable discussing topics in Dr. Neeley's area of responsibility."

"I understand Verna. Just a simple question. How is the Labrador and how is he doing?"

"You can talk to Dr. Neeley, doctor, but I can tell you this much. The dog was sacrificed several days ago."

"A perfectly healthy, young Lab was sacrificed?"

"Dr. Neeley said to me that it was an equipment failure --- an electrical short electrocuted the dog --- he said."

"Verna, I am shocked that you believe that lie. Corbin implanted some electromagnetic widget that killed an otherwise healthy animal."

"Oh, my goodness, you are frightening me, Dr. Hertzmann. Please stop."

"It should scare you to death, Verna. Did you observe him put the animal in the cremation furnace?"

"No, I have no responsibilities related to the cremation furnace, doctor."

"Do you know that the animal's death was ascertained before he put it in the furnace?"

"No, I hope Dr. Neeley would never deliberately sacrifice any animal that he could have saved."

"I'll learn the details when I confront Dr. Neeley with such an outrage. Thank you for telling me about this. I do want to say another thing to you, Verna. Policies here at Azran Clinic discourage romantic interaction between employees."

Verna's upper lip curled into a snare. "Why are you threatening me, Dr. Hertzmann?"

"Employees remark about you and Dr. Neeley and your job could be in jeopardy."

"Is this confidential information you want to hear? You are mistaken and it is unprofessional for you to even ask such questions." Verna started to leave the coffee room shaking her head from side to side.

"One final question, Verna." Gunter leaned closer and placed his hand on her shoulder speaking softly into her ear. "I'm sorry, Verna. I apologize --- and, now tell me what disposition was made of the dog --- if you will, please."

"In the cremation furnace as usual, of course, Dr. Hertzmann exactly as we discussed just minutes ago."

"Okay, Verna, thank you. We are still friends, aren't we?"

"Sure we are!" She stuck her tongue out as she walked away.

CHAPTER 7

L'OMMIES WATERING HOLE

Corbin Neeley met Verna at L'Ommies in Mt. View for a confidential talk and cocktails. L'Ommies was the watering hole and meat market for young aspiring executives, older, on-the-prowl men from Los Altos Hills and always several of the white shoe, ex-execs from Hillsborough farther up the peninsula closer to South San Francisco.

L'Ommies was always a hubbub of loud talking suits, business conversations over lunch or dinner or drunken blathering at the bar. Dinner patrons often had several drinks at the bar before transferring to their dining tables and in most cases were rarely able to overhear any conversations at other tables. Too, L'Ommies waiters or waitresses had learned or been trained to turn a deaf ear to any personal conversations whether about business or budding, amorous affairs. Any of L'Ommie's employees failing to abide by that code were summarily dismissed on site.

Corbin had selected this location for exactly these reasons. It was far too noisy for anyone at nearby tables to hear private conversations and people in L'Ommies were too caught up in their own egos to be interested in idle chatter at other tables.

Corbin had reached for Verna's hand several times and been rebuffed with a shrug of her shoulders and a hushed, unintelligible mumble.

"Corbin", she said, "Dr. Hertzmann wants me to report you to Dr. Azran and Gunter said to tell Dr. Azran that you are doing experimental animal surgeries."

"Verna, what I am doing can improve your life, bring you happiness and a state of mind that is so marvelous and such a euphoric stimulant--- you must try to understand."

"No, I do not understand. You have violated my body; I have felt only pain and one of the most frightening incidents of my life. And, Corbin, I do not need to understand." Verna spits out words like a cobra spitting venom.

"But, just minor enhancements will eliminate the discomfort and you will actually enjoy how you feel. I promise you." Dr. Neeley touched her cheek.

"Don't touch me, Corbin." Verna's lips twisted into a grotesque snarl.

"Please, Verna, just listen. Let me explain the beautiful potential to you." Verna's expression did not change.

"I have implanted a multiple wave oscillator temporarily in your uterus. It is a simple sound generator that is powered by the isotonic fluids in your body. It is a completely natural and safe method that should not make you afraid. This device can generate, multiple frequencies and stimulate strong, healthy emotions that are totally under your own control."

"Corbin! I am not sick, at least, I was fine until you used me like a guinea pig or one of your lab rats."

"Please, Verna. Let me finish. Whenever you want the instrument explanted, I will do it but, first just hear what I am saying. For instance, sore knees or torn muscles can be placed inside magnetic fields for a few, short minutes at a time, helping to heal much faster than conventional medications or things like clumsy Tens systems."

"I will say it again, Corbin. I am or was not sick until you raped--- yes, raped is the word --- raped me."

Corbin reached for his glass and as it teetered precariously on the edge of the table, he made an awkward grab at it, knocking the Cabernet to the floor. After too many glasses, he was oblivious to the spilled wine.

"I want to show you the beauty of this. The device is capable of various sound frequencies; not all frequencies are audible to the human ear. I can show you how to select and control these frequencies easily and simply. Understand that eleven Hertz, that is 11 cycles per second, cannot be heard with our ears. However, such frequencies can produce a spectrum of emotions. Let me explain for just another minute or so --- the body will sympathize or to put it another way, the body can enjoy Delta waves and the body will profoundly relax, lower pain and cut emotional distress. Such a wonderful frequency will also initiate the flow of melatonin-inducing sleep. Do you know what I am saying, Verna"

"I can, Corbin. I am not as dumb as you may think. What do you mean by "hurts"?"

"Oh, yes, the term H E R T Z means or is the same as CPS, that is cycles per second. See, Delta is a low frequency. Theta is between 3.3 and 7.8 cps which induce a dream state, trance--- even allows rapid learning or self-hypnosis. Next, Alpha waves are 7.8 to 14 cps inducing relaxation, meditation, healing, etc. like a comfortable state. Then, Beta waves is the higher frequencies 14 to 30 Hz create feelings of stimulation, energizing or intensifying. Verna, I can see from your bewildered expression that you either do not understand or you just cannot comprehend such technicalities whatsoever."

"That is not a correct interpretation you are making, Corbin. I did understand the scientific mumbo-jumbo knowing that you are trying to divert my mind to act like I enjoy you surgical tinkering on my body."

"No, Verna, not in the least. I do care for you. Maybe, I am falling in love. Simply put without all the electrical brain wave details, I truly want you to experience physical and mental stimulations far in excess of the majority of any other humans. Your health and comforts are the foundations of everything important and vital to me."

"Is this true, Corbin. Is this fact or just your wild imagination?" Verna actually smiled. Her third Dirty Martini was mellowing her judgment.

"Absolute fact, Verna. You may have heard that high voltage power lines set up a magnetic field. Well, it is felt that such magnetism can harm people who live near such power lines. However, it is a matter of frequencies, do you see?"

"If I ask you to take this gadget out of me, will you do it when I say --- immediately?"

"Of course, Verna. I care for you. I can limit the device to extremely low frequencies, that is, ELF frequencies, to correspond to certain brain frequencies and at the first sign of any discomfort whatsoever, I will remove it."

"What about what happened to me at the grocery?"

"That was some piece of equipment in the store that gave off interfering signals. The result was a heterodyne effect. It will not happen when I adjust the wave oscillator."

"One week, Corbin! One incident of any kind and I will tell everything to Dr. Azran."

CHAPTER 8

MAURICE'S RESTAURANT

Nearly hidden in the Los Altos foothills, Maurice's French Restaurant was well known from Los Angeles to San Francisco for uniquely superb specialties from a world class chef.

Alex Bondurant and Carlton Herrick had arrived early to talk prior to the arrival of the Biotherm attorney, Hale Irving, J.D., who had been corporate legal counsel for the past five years.

"When Hale gets here, Carlton, you begin with your concerns about Gigatrax Ltd. and I will join in with my thoughts." Alex was calm and collected usually but this evening, he seemed uncomfortable.

"Well, Alex, I have a lot of concerns and I am anxious to hear Hale's counsel. Incidentally, I'll order the drinks if you are ready."

"Go ahead if you want something now. Hale will be here shortly. I'll wait for him."

"Me, too."

Hale Irving arrived at the next moment. "Hello Alex. How are you, Carlton? I haven't seen you in several weeks, maybe longer."

"Good to see you again, Hale. May I order you a drink?"

"Maybe better if we talk about the latest business concerns first."

"Fine. You will recall Gigatrax Ltd. has made overtures about various cooperative ventures with Biotherm."

"And," Alex added," there was the talk of attracting me away from Biotherm to join Gigatrax Ltd. in some executive capacity."

"First, we need to focus on the salient points. All we have so far is rumors that usually can't justify much concern."

A young waiter interrupted the conversation.

"Gentlemen, can I interest you in a drink?"

"Can you tell us first what you recommend for dinner?" Carlton asked.

"Of course, tonight we are serving muse-asparagus with shitake and lemon cream. It is excellent or I can strongly recommend grilled squab with wild rice risotto. I have heard good compliments on our muse-asparagus."

Alex smacked his lips asking, "So, in your personal opinion. What is best on or off the menu this evening, Garcon?"

"Yessir, my absolute favorite here at Maurice's is the Vichyssoise; it is sheer ambrosia."

All three ordered dinner and awaited the next response from Alex Bondurant.

"You two go ahead and order a drink, but I will pass tonight."

Carlton returned to the business discussion. "Gigatrax Ltd. may be scheming to take control of Biotherm. They have patents that could be enhanced if some of Biotherm's patents were added to their balance sheet. Conversely, if Biotherm had those Gigatrax Ltd. patents, Biotherm's financial strength would be significantly improved."

"Well, Carlton, from the positions you have just described, a merger, at least, a joint venture could be attractive to both companies, but please continue."

Carlton hesitated before responding, "From my personal view, I would prefer not to be subordinate to Max Becker who is Gigatrax Ltd. President and CEO."

Alex interrupted, "Hale, I'll begin with an assumption that Gigatrax Ltd. has been approached by a world conglomerate, possibly, the EU Research Funding group. As you know, the Euro is being hit hard and most countries under the EU can and will pay exorbitant Euros to absorb an American company with a high technology product line."

"Well," Hale added, "if Gigatrax Ltd. can butter their balance sheet ---."

"And," Carlton pointed out, "control of Biotherm with our strong patents and our successful technologies would make Gigatrax Ltd. highly attractive."

Alex commented, "Yes, Carlton and I have had guarded discussion with our Board of Directors and no apparent survival strategy has been developed."

"Gentlemen," Hale interrupted." your present focus is mistakenly aimed in the wrong direction. You should be taking advantage of opportunities rather than on personalities."

Carlton reached across the dining table to place his hand on Hale's wrist. "Explain that last remark, Hale. It sounds like you are headed into the center of our problems. So, please, go ahead."

"Okay, first, defer all thoughts and references about Max Becker. I am suggesting that we pinpoint our discussion tonight on the pluses and positive aspects exclusively." Hale made his point by slapping his hand on the table.

Alex had been nodding his head in agreement. "Then, Hale, what is the most significant position that Biotherm might take?"

"Both Biotherm and Gigatrax have outstanding growth potential. Biotherm is potentially a hand-in-glove fit as an acquisition by Gigatrax. Concurrently, Gigatrax, obviously, would make a tremendous asset if acquired by Biotherm. This is clearly an excellent joint venture opportunity."

"I understand your point, Hale." Carlton commented, "give me the bottom line anyway."

"From my perspective, a well planned merger is in the best interest of both companies. It is potential, a win-win situation for everyone."

"Appreciate you sound logic, Hale. Of course, the senior executives from both companies could easily lay out the perfect merger ---." Alex was nodding agreement and smiling.

"Exactly, Alex, over a dinner just like we are doing tonight."

Hale motioned for the waiter. "I could use that drink at this point, gentlemen."

The meeting was continued as drinks were ordered. Hale had some pertinent questions.

"Alex and you, too, Carlton, I want you to tell me where is the power at Gigatrax, who makes final executive decisions and who is the heir apparent in event of any management change."

"I can answer that readily," Alex chimed in, "Max Becker is the honcho and controls every decision even well before the Board is involved."

Carlton pointed his index finger toward the ceiling and said, "I'd agree but I really do not know Max. However, I'd say the potential powerhouse and maybe, heir apparent is K. B. Randall. Before joining Gigatrax, a little bio search on LinkedIn revealed that K. B. was a CPA who went back to law school and later as a J.D. built a reputation as a District Attorney."

Hale nodded his head acknowledging Carlton's opinion. "I know her by reputation and she is tough-minded. I'd guess with her as second in command, Max Becker has all his bases covered. But, I have a more important question. What interactions occur between you, Alex and Max Becker?"

"We don't socialize, Hale, if that is the question."

Hale turned his attention to Carlton. "Carlton, do you know K. B. Randall?

"I do know of her."

"Then, how well do you know her? I can guess she has full knowledge of every move past, present or future for Gigatrax." Hale stated.

"I do understand," Carlton said, "but I'm anxious to hear the next questions."

"First, do either of you and any Gigatrax Ltd. executives belong to any of the same professional or social organization --- even church?"

Alex and Carlton answered no with a shake of their heads.

"Now, I will earn the fine dinner Biotherm has provided me tonight. Every year Gigatrax Ltd. and Biotherm attend an expensive meeting of the Bio-Instrumentation Academy. Am I correct?"

"Yes, we do, Hale, and you are correct; it is expensive," Alex answered.

"Okay, this is a perfect opportunity to interact, gather competitive data, see any new technologies and a vital chance to spend coffee breaks, lunches or dinners with competitors or potential competitors. Alex you might consider attending this year's meeting. Where is it held this year?"

"New Orleans. It is scheduled for next month in fact. I am planning to be there."

"Alex, call Max Becker and arrange a dinner meeting in one of the better, upscale restaurants. Carlton, I suggest that you e-mail K. B. Randall ---then call her --- the same concept. She is still young. Take her to Pascal Manale's. Have a great dinner or the best oysters in the city. The potential, competitive info to be gained can be of real value, of course."

Carlton stood up excusing himself. "Hale, thanks for the wise counsel. I totally agree it is a workable idea and your suggestion for dinner at Pascal Manale's. I was there two years ago and still remember the excellent food."

Hale and Alex both stood in preparation for leaving.

"Evening well spent gentlemen," Carlton said as he shook hands with Hale, "and, Alex, see you in the morning."

CHAPTER 9

GIGATRAX BOARD MEETING

G igatrax Ltd. corporate facility was a sprawling maze of seven buildings located in a burgeoning city in the East Bay of San Francisco called Walnut Creek. The administrative building was occupied by the accounting department, marketing, sales, advertising\promotion, legal, medical affairs as well as the offices of the senior executives. On the northeast corner of the building, a large conference room caught the morning and afternoon sun, and it was this room where the Board of Directors met quarterly. This morning the Board had been in discussion for over two hours. Max Becker was conducting a power point presentation with every projection boldly marked Company Confidential for Board Members Exclusively.

Max Becker stood a formidable six foot two, vibrantly healthy and a regular at the Triathlon Athletic Club for a heavy cardiovascular work. Max had the same breakfast every morning, sixteen ounces of a crushed iced drink containing blueberries, yogurt, protein powder, a spoonful of blackstrap molasses, brewer's yeast and topped with a teaspoon of cayenne pepper. His day at Gigatrax began precisely at eight thirty every morning.

Max brought the same energy and commitment to his business affairs, and this morning he captured a high-interest level with his Board of Directors.

K. B. Randall studied the faces of the other board members around the conference table, assessed their individual attitudes as well as mentally reviewing the business personality of each one. K. B. had already forecasted the result of today's vote on the Biotherm acquisition. All eyes focused on K. B. as she slowly eased her chair away from the table, standing to demonstrate her intended control of the discussion. Her voluptuous manner and the sexually evocative body were more than enough to capture the attention of every male on the board of directors. She sauntered to the head of the conference table without announcement. She hesitated a long time before turning and facing the other board members.

"Each of you, gentlemen, know my position and perspective on the acquisition of Biotherm."

"Yes, but---" The interruption came from Fred Terman. Fred had been on the board for three years and was the founder\owner of a very prestigious consulting firm that provided expert opinions on matters of medical and regulatory affairs.

K. B. snapped her attention directly to Terman.

"I am eager to hear your position on this matter, Fred, if you can postpone your expensive opinions until I complete my comments."

"Of course, K. B." Terman waited until she turned and took several steps in another direction before admiring her long, supple legs and her perfectly contoured posterior.

"Alright," K. B. quipped, "as a fiscally conscientious exec and as the chief financial officer, I want it clearly understood that any attempt at a hostile takeover will be financially ill-advised."

"Fine, K. B., but I don't see that." Terman harrumphed.

"Let me put it this way, Fred. If we have to bribe Biotherm stockholders to gain a majority position, we will need lots of clout and plenty of cash. R & D on our new anticholinergic drug would be lethally curtailed. It is that simple."

K. B. walked around the table touching each board member on the shoulder before settling again in her own chair.

Silence followed and lots of water glasses were refilled. Two of the younger board members poured themselves fresh, hot coffee. Kenny McMasters poured his coffee and spilled half the cup onto the serving table. McMasters is President and CEO of a growing bioscience company called Genomix located in South San Francisco. He spun around too quickly and sloshed most of the coffee remaining in his cup.

"K. B., no surprise in hearing your fiscal perspective. That's how you earn the big bucks."

His half-pointed remark incited a muffled laugh around the table.

"But," he continued, "Gigatrax Ltd. needs the product line expansion, the demonstrated research skills of Biotherm and --- hey --- the eighteen solid patents on the Biotherm balance sheet."

K. B. starting to stand again said, "So, Ken, when the cash crunch comes, we can depend on a cash infusion from Genomics, right?"

"Sit back down, K. B., and relax. Hear me out on this, okay?"

She sat down crossing her tanned legs for maximum effect.

"Roll on sweet Avon," she said with a reluctant smile.

Fred Terman slid his chair away from the conference table and began tapping his head with his index finger. "Okay, K. B. here is my thinking. Backburner the hostile takeover thinking. Focus on some other method to fold Biotherm in. Even early concerns regarding rumors of a hostile takeover can drain operating capital --- certainly, add some bad numbers to the balance sheet. If Genomics initiated such a rumor mill, Gigatrax Ltd. might be able to swoop in and take control of Biotherm. Any other thoughts?"

"Uh-huh, we can offer to extend the morning coffee breaks --- maybe, free donuts and pastries. Biotherm labor force will race to get on our payroll." K. B. poured herself another cup of coffee.

Max Becker tossed his pen onto the paperwork in front of him and pointed to the clock.

"Enough, boys and girls. Can we get back to the matter on the table? This matter needs board approval, and the approved strategy needs to be put into an action plan like immediately. Am I clear?"

All heads acknowledged the dictates just issued by the boss.

"Fred, I think your concept has merit. You and I can detail a plan privately." K. B. nodded her appreciation.

"Okay, sure. First, we plant innuendoes around town, in and out of the plant here, rumoring that Gigatrax Ltd. wants to recruit Alex Bondurant away from Biotherm, and bring him into Gigatrax Ltd. as Chairman."

"And ---"

"And, that Gigatrax Ltd. is interested in a cooperative venture with Biotherm."

"Uh-huh, so far, I like the strategy." K. B. flashed her best Hollywood smile.

The smile was contagious around the table.

"My point is that if we can affect a clean, cooperative merger ---- even just a genuine cooperative venture, Gigatrax Ltd. stock, as well as Biotherm's, will bounce eight to ten points up --- maybe more."

Max Becker tapped vigorously on his laptop, and stated, "K. B. ---"

"Yes, sir." She responded.

"How quickly can you get me a spreadsheet showing an addition of four million shares of Class A Preferred ---- ah --- using two dollars under market as of last Friday?"

"Can you give me twenty minutes, Max?"

"And, I want financial projections through fiscal 2020, okay?"

"How about one hour, boss?"

"Let's call it 1:30 after lunch today. Now, I want each of you to subtly let it be known that Gigatrax Ltd. is preparing to make an offer to Alex Bondurant --- no details --- just that."

"How do you want to spin it, Max?" Fred Terman's question came with a frown.

"Do it your own way. I don't want a pat story. It's better if no two rumors match. If the story is too structured, it loses credibility. Use your imagination."

"And, one more thing, K. B. Are you planning to go to the Bio-Instrumentation meeting in New Orleans?"

"Well, no. Actually, Max, I was hoping to take a few days of vacation during that same period. The marketing and sales people will be out of my hair, and I'll have some breathing room."

"Good, take some extra, private time in New Orleans. Make sure you will be seen with Alex Bondurant. And, K. B., get to know Carlton Herrick. That may be very important. Herrick has a big influence on Alex and on the Biotherm board. Herrick is the heir apparent at Biotherm."

"I understand, but what do you ---what do we need to know about Herrick? I've heard some wild stories about Herrick."

"No stories here today, K. B. We will talk details after lunch."

CHAPTER 10

THEFT AT AZRAN CLINIC

On Wednesday morning, Carlton's alarm aroused him at 5: 30 AM reminding him to get dressed quickly and follow his plan at the Azran Clinic for Exotic and Febrile disease. Totally out of character, he selected an old, wrinkled pair of chino jeans. He chose a faded pullover sweat-shirt with a hood to cover his face if he felt it the best decision. He finished dressing without making a sound and left the house through the garage door. His car had been left parked on the street to keep early morning noise to a minimum.

Mentally reviewing his plan and the details of the morning activities at Azran Clinic, he drove at a speed that would put him within one block of the Azran Clinic shipping and receiving dock. Within seconds of his targeted arrival time, he parked on a side street precisely the space he had used in the previous trial runs.

The shipping and receiving dock was in the rear of building number 3; the walk would put him there at 7:00. Typically, several night shift workers used this exit and had their cars parked in the back lot.

Carlton remained under the dock with good visibility of the rear door. Minutes after 7: 08 the usual employees had left the building and driven away. Carlton was at the door and inside in less than 15 seconds. Seeing a lab coat left behind by one of the departing employees, he put it on and walked confidently toward Dr. Azran's office. Surprised and not expecting, the door to be locked, he stood nonchalantly with his back against the wall with a broom in his hand. He watched both directions down the hallway as he removed a credit card from his wallet. Slipping the card between the door frame and the lock and he was almost in as someone called from down the hall.

"Hey, when you get done there, I need some trash swept up down here in my office."

Carlton gave the broom a little shake and mumbled an indistinguishable "uh-huh" as he walked into Azran's office and closed the door behind him. With the skill of an experienced burglar, he went through Azran's desk until he located a box of business cards. Opening the box confirmed the cards as belonging to Azran. He removed a small stack and as he placed the lid back on, the remaining cards fell to the floor behind the desk. From the bottom right drawer, he removed a box of Azran's personal, letterhead stationery and put it into the waste can.

The office door flew open and the voice from down the hall asked, "When you gonna' be done here? I'll wait down in my office."

As Carlton picked up the waste can under Azran's desk he garbled a reply, "Five minutes".

Azran's office inter-connected with the doctor's lounge. Carlton went in straight to Azran's locker. He found a lab coat with blue embroidery over the left pocket. In large letters --- Harman Azran, M.D., Ph.D.

Carlton grabbed the waste can and held the lab coat under his arm, Azran's business cards in his pocket, he sauntered toward the rear door, tucked the box of letterheads under his arm, dumped the waste can in the dumpster and walked back to his car.

His drive back home was uneventful. Carlton felt like he had just won the Nobel Prize for shrewdness. His plan was smoother than twenty-year-old Scotch.

The sanctuary of home felt good and he was back already having his morning coffee and reviewing his successes. Carlton was hungry for a big breakfast as a reward for bravery and gallantry. This morning the hot coffee seemed most adequate and he relished just relaxing in his kitchen all alone.

He poured his third cup of coffee and started thinking about the next step in his plan. He remembered the political chaos at Biotherm and the threat of Gigatrax Ltd. take over. His confidence sent him a subliminal message telling him he was and will always be a winner.

"Well, good morning, early bird. You taking the day off today. I didn't even hear you get up this morning." Alyssa Herrick, his wife, a sprightly blonde that looked like she spent lots of time at the health club doing Pilates and things to keep her young body healthy and vivacious had just whisked into the room.

"No, honey. I didn't want to wake you. I have an important presentation today for the Board and needed some private time to think."

"Carlton, it reminds me when you were really happy and once and awhile would get up before the sun and go fishing."

"Well, Alyssa, your memory is much better than mine. All I can remember is what I had for breakfast ---- speaking of which, I missed breakfast this morning."

"Easy problem to solve, hon. Gimme' ten minutes and magically before you will appear eggs, bacon, biscuits, and gravy; just like back home in Cairo, Illinois."

Carlton leaned back in his swivel chair and spilled his coffee down the front of his pull-over sweater. "I have no memories of living in Illinois. That was a hundred years ago but, I gotta' get to the office."

Alyssa laughed. "In those grubby clothes? Why did you put those on this morning?"

"Tell you tonight, honey. Bye-bye."

"--- and Juliette called very early this morning before 7 AM; didn't leave a message."

CHAPTER 11

UPS IMPOSSIBLE SCAM

Traffic on the Bayshore was still slow moving even after the earlier morning traffic rush to work. Carlton activated his VOX operated car phone announcing, "Call office."

Juliette answered in milliseconds, "Good morning, Mr. Herrick's office, this is Juliette."

"I'm in heavy traffic on Bloody Bayshore and I will be in the office around nine sometimes. Get me whatever info you can find on the Communicable Disease Center in Perth, Australia ---- things like addresses, phone numbers, senior scientists and, give me the same kind of portfolio on CDC in Atlanta. Oh, 0h --- looks like a fender bender up ahead. I better call you later".

Carlton's eight-cylinder Jaguar had almost memorized the routing to the Azran Clinic from the repeated trips over the past several weeks. He patted his loaded briefcase now containing Azran's lab coat, business cards and a dozen or so letterheads with the impressive logo "Azran Clinic for Exotic and Febrile Disease."

He parked the Jaguar far back in the lot in the least conspicuous spot hidden behind an RV, an old pickup truck, several stacks of cardboard boxes, and other disposable materials. Carlton could feel his pulse rate quickening and he took a deep breath to compose himself. Before opening the car door, he scanned the entire back lot and as much as he could see of the loading dock. The UPS deliveries came in from the northeast corner of the lot. From that corner, he had calculated the time for the UPS truck to reach the loading dock. He removed the lab coat from his briefcase and unfolded it in preparation.

At exactly 7:30, he got out of the car and stood tall smelling the freshness of the morning air. He continued to survey the parking area before reaching back into the car to grab the lab coat. He jumped from hearing a door slam in the space next to him. He tossed the lab coat back into the car and spun around finding himself within touching distance of a uniformed man with a package under his arm.

"Say there. Are you one of the docs here in this hospital?"

Carlton quickly regained his composure and laughed. "I wish. Hell no. I work for the sanitation department. You know, trash pick-up, and stuff like that."

"Sorry to bother you. I'm here looking for a person. Nice car! Yours?"

"No way. I pick it up every week for wash and detail. Wish it was mine 'tho. Are you a sheriff or something?"

"No, uniform gets me in places easier. I'm delivering a court summons. Glad it ain't you."

"Yeah, me too, but How come you park way the hell back here?"

"Easy question, when you are serving a summons, you don't get invited in for coffee and donuts."

"Right, I should have known that. I am glad your summons is not for me."

The uniformed process server nodded and sauntered toward the loading dock.

Carlton got back into his car to catch his breath and slow down his racing heart. Checking his watch, he noted it was almost 8:03. The lost seventeen minutes wasted talking to the process server seemed like half a lifetime. At 8:20, the uniformed man returned to his car and drove away. Carlton retrieved the lab coat and glanced around as he put it on.

Carlton began slowly walking toward the loading dock. Just after 8:24, the UPS entered the back lot. Carlton increased his pace to put him directly in the path of the delivery truck. With his back toward the UPS driver, he listened for the sound of the truck engine. The driver hit the horn twice as he slowed the vehicle to a near stop. Carlton turned around with his most gregarious smile and as he approached the truck, he gave a welcome wave to the driver. Carlton held up his hand, palm forward, to stop the truck and get immediate attention from the driver. The driver rolled down his window nodding and looking directly down at the person in the white lab coat.

"Oh, Dr. Azran --- didn't mean to blow my horn at you. I didn't know who you were." The driver's eyes kept staring at the bold, blue embroidery on the lab coat that read Harman Azran, M.D., Ph.D.

"No problem, young man. I'm Dr. Azran and I am expecting an extremely important shipment. Glad I met you this morning."

"Nice to meet you Dr. Azran but I don't have any delivery for you today but, I'll keep my eyes open for it."

"I will appreciate that very much. In fact, I would like to ask you for a very, personal favor ---"

The UPS driver grinned as he spoke, "Well, of course, Dr. Ozran, you are one of our UPS favorites and whatever you need, I will make it happen. Anyway, doctor, what is it you need?"

"The name is a little difficult. Sounds like you may have been thinking about Dr. OZ. Azran is my name. No matter, just doc is fine, whatever gets my attention".

"I do apologize for that doc. So, what can I do for you?"

"I am doing some private, very confidential studies and the package I'm expecting is vital for my work and is very important. If you would call me on my personal number, I'll know when to meet you here in the rear delivery area."

"You got it, doc. Tell me the right number to call."

Carlton penciled a number on a scrap of paper, saying, "Here you go." They both nodded as they shook hands.

The truck headed toward the loading dock. Carlton headed back toward his car removing the coat and folding it to pack into his briefcase.

CHAPTER 12

LETTERS TO CDC

At 5 AM, the Biotherm parking lot was a vacant expanse of blacktop with the morning dew evaporating toward the morning sun. Carlton Herrick drove around the building surveying for any other early employees. As he returned to the executive parking area, he opened his briefcase removing the Azran business cards and letterhead. A single page of letterhead was placed under the sun visor, the balance was tucked into a red file folder marked private and confidential. For an inordinate time, he smiled as he studied one of the business cards. He placed the rest of the business cards in his shirt pocket. The sun was beginning to shine through the passenger side window as he pulled down the sun visor and focused on the letterhead from the Azran Clinic for Exotic and Febrile Disease.

Carlton nodded his head with self-adulation. His plan was running just as he had laid it out. "Smooth, smooth --- smooth", he lip-synched.

Two taps on the car window. Carlton's heart quickened. Open-mouthed, he turned his head to the sound at the window.

A broad smile exposing nicotine stained teeth leaned into the window knocking once more. "Good morning, Mr. Carlton. Did'ja knows it's the early bird that gets the worm?"

Carlton stammered for a response as he rolled down the window and folded the letterhead. "Scared the hell outta me, Jessie. I got a big presentation this morning. The bird with the best preparation gets the worm always."

"Yes sir, Mr. Herrick. You betcha".

"Jessie, what time you come on duty every morning?"

"Well, I try to be on the lot by 5 o'clock, but just a few minutes late this morning." Jessie smiled again showing his yellow, picket fence teeth and walked away bobbing his head side to side.

Carlton enjoyed the morning solitude of his office. He dictated a letter which would be mailed to the Communicable Disease Center in Atlanta, Georgia and a second communication to the Communicable Disease Center in New South Wales, Australia. A note attached to the cassette instructed Juliette to type the two letters, one to Dr. Boynton and the other to Dr. Rogers at CDC in Atlanta.

Carlton searched his Blackberry for previously recorded notes on his plan to eliminate Max Becker and grease his slide into Executive Vice President when Gigatrax Ltd. swallows up Biotherm. Carlton reviewed each entry point by point before continuing his draft to the Communicable Disease Center.

Elaine Boynton, M.D., Ph.D., Sc.D.
100 Clifton Road
Atlanta, GA 30333

My Esteemed Colleague Dr. Boynton:
Congratulations on your recent publication in the August Journal of Epidemiology. You may recall our meeting last year at the American College of Epidemiology meeting in Chicago. My work on various Enterobacteriaceae is an interesting parallel to the impressive studies you have done on streptococcal gangrene. However, I plan to publish more extensively on Beta hemolytic streptococci. I would be humbled should you be willing to work with me on a collaborative study. Flesh eating bacteria responsible for necrotizing fasciitis is an area of investigation that should easily find grant money from the National Institutes of Health.
Please ship me lyophilized cultures of two of your cultures, viz., S. pyogenes and C. perfringenes. Clostridium has become big business. If women using Botox understood the active ingredient to be C. botulinum, the manufacturers stock would drop. Who might have guessed that botulism would be for sale!
Please package the cultures appropriately with brown paper wrapping and do ship to me marked Personal and Confidential. This study is unannounced here at the clinic. I much prefer to limit all such communication between the two of us.
Please include a note in the package if you are possibly interested in some collaborative effort on C. hyicus or C. novyi.

Respectfully yours,
~~Harman Azran, M.D., Ph.D.~~ Julie, Leave this blank.

The letters were completed and on Carlton's desk within the hour.

Along with the letters, Juliette had sealed a penciled memo in an envelope marked FOR YOUR EYES ONLY. It read as follow:

Carlton,

I suspect that we need to talk privately before moving ahead with whatever madness you have conjured up. It is far from apparent to me where you are headed, but I do feel it vital that we discuss my genuine concern that the risks may outweigh the imagined results.

Too, you know that Alex is aging and it is also known that he has angina or some serious heart problem. My point is that you, without a doubt, will be bumped up by the board to Pres.\CEO in the event something happens to him.

Then, again, all this may be none of my business or just as likely too complex for my understanding. Anyway, whatever you are thinking may be premature or just ill-advised.

Juliette

Carlton read the penciled note several times. First, he thought it a personal affront that Julie could have the audacity reading, his conclusion changed to a mental illusion of himself sitting in Alex's office with no one to question his seasoned, executive experience. After, the next keys to the corporate kingdom --- whatever that meant. A third conclusion, evolved after the third reading. This time, the innate personality of Carlton R. Herrick, Jr. morphed into a better concept. He felt that any opinion Juliette had was unrelated and not germane to the complex matters that he faced. His logic stepped in and reminded him of his mental faux pas that Julie already had tangible evidence of potentially immoral or illegal consequences. Therefore, acknowledging Julie's suggestions and complimenting her on her keen business acuity was obviously the best route to circumvent any complications. He nodded his head in self-admiration of his own mixture of flattery and good judgment.

He folded the letters and placed them and the business cards from his pocket into his red portfolio which he locked in his desk drawer.

Next, he sent a text message to Julie telling her that her comments were excellent and showed him again why he had picked her as his personal administrative aide. He added an idea that dinner and a fine bottle of some exquisite wine would allow them to relax and discuss the entire thing in greater detail.

As he prepared to leave his office, he turned to look at the row after row of cubicles where all the grunts and peons worked at their meaningless, insignificant jobs.

He entered Juliette's cubicle. "Did you get my text note?"

"Yes, and yes," she whispered, "great idea."

"Me too. Can't agree more than that. But, I got I got a very early jump on priorities for today. Meeting for business brunch in San Francisco. Got to leave now. --- should be back after one o'clock."

Carlton stepped back into his office and extracted the red portfolio deciding to mail both CDC letters from the San Francisco post office. He reviewed both letters and made a few notes for himself. He attempted to sign both using Dr. Azran's signature which he had copied from another piece of correspondence taken from Azran's desk.

CHAPTER 13

K. B. CONTACTS CARLTON

At 10 o'clock, Carlton was having his third cup of black coffee and studying technical papers and scientific books on toxicology. Alyssa came into the kitchen from the back patio surprised to see Carlton still home. "Carlton, you have been drinking more and more coffee. That cannot be good for you."

"I know that Alyssa. With all the problems at Biotherm, I need something to keep my sanity."

"Well, Carlton, your sanity has never been in question, but if you get a heart attack, your sanity won't be at blame. Anyway, how many cups have you had this morning? And, speaking of the morning which is slipping away, are you going to the office today?"

"Of course, I may get home later than usual today ---". His cell phone rang; he recognized the special ring as coming from his office. It was unusual for Julie Vissetti to call him at home even if he was running late.

"Mr. Herrick, I'm sorry to have to call you at home. I apologize but a call came in early this morning from Gigatrax Ltd. from someone in the accounting department. I accepted the call and was immediately transferred to one of the senior execs, a girl called K. B. but I explained that you were in conference and had instructed me not to interrupt the meeting."

She said, "That's okay, "I wanted to ask when he might be flying to the Bio-Instrumentation meeting in New Orleans."

"It is not on his agenda," I said, "but I think it will be Thursday or Friday next week."

"Have him call me," she said, "It is rather important. He knows the number."

"Thank you, Julie. I will be there before noon. Will you check with Marcella and find out when and if Alex is planning to go to New Orleans and when he plans to leave?"

Alyssa listened to Carlton's asking Julie about New Orleans. "Is Julie going to New Orleans?"

"No, she isn't. I asked her to talk to Marcella to find out when Alex is planning to leave."

"Will you be flying with Alex?"

"No, Alex is some kind of pessimist or maybe he is a fatalist. He does not want the two of us on the same flight. In fact, he would prefer that we not be on the same airline together. I really don't mind. I get a lot more work done when I am not barraged with questions or casual conversation. It gets tiring sometimes."

"Speaking of tired, Carlton. You have been looking a bit worn down for the last week or two. Why not take the day off today. It is almost half gone already. We can have a nice lunch together on the patio and take a swim together."

"Sounds like a good idea, Alyssa but I can't do it today. Way too much preparation to do for the Bio-Instrumentation meeting. When I get back home from New Orleans, we can take a few days just for ourselves --- and, ah, maybe act like we are kids again."

"Shall I hold my breath? Anyway, how about some lunch before you run back to your Biotherm home?"

"Gotta' go, Alyssa but thanks for the offer."

Carlton pulled away from his garage and took Page Mill Road to connect to 101. The Jaguar was as close as he had come to a really upscale sports car. The Jaguar was fine when he bought it five years ago but it was a bit too much playboy now and his big ambition was to own a classical Bentley with a more executive look than any sports car. He fumbled with his address book on the car's phone system looking for Gigatrax Ltd. phone number. He reached the computerized answering system at Gigatrax and spoke "K. B. Randall".

"This is K. B. You must be driving with a window down. The sound of rushing air reveals the secret."

"Surprised at getting your call earlier. I suppose we know each other better by reputation than personally or from business interaction. What can I do for you?"

"Carlton, I'm not on an espionage assignment. To the contrary, with all the wild rumors floating around the Peninsula, I decided we should talk informally about areas of mutual interest."

"That is fine with me K. B. It is just that I get edgy talking to women with J.D. after their names."

"Don't let the J.D. thing make you edgy. I'm strictly a business person now."

"I would like to meet you face to face and see if we can erase some of the vicious stories floating around. Where would you like to meet and does everyone call you K. B.?"

"Sometimes I'm called lots worse. I believe we are both going to the Bio-Instrumentation exhibits in New Orleans. Why don't we fly there together?"

"The long flight will allow us to talk about anything and I think it is a good idea. Can you email me your flight plans and possibly, I can still get on the same plane."

"Better yet, Carlton. I will make reservations for both of us and make it easier to get on the same plane at the same time."

"Good. I can cover my airfare costs to you or to Gigatrax by PayPal if you like."

"That's perfect Carlton. I am anxious to spend some time getting to know you. I have heard complimentary stories about you and I'd like to learn if they are true."

"Believe nothing you hear, K. B. and I'll be in touch with you in the next day or so."

"My private Googol number is 415 555-2222. You need not go through the Gigatrax phone system. I'm looking forward to the trip with you."

"Me too, K. B., one question for planning purposes. Got one more minute, K. B.?"

"Of course, pro bono to you Carlton."

"Do you know New Orleans, K. B.?"

"As a matter of fact, I do know New Orleans, at least, the French Quarter."

"Do you have a favorite food or know a favorite place for dinner in New Orleans?'

"Not exactly. I'm just not a big fan of Red Beans and Rice. How about you?"

"Since you asked, I know of a place in Uptown New Orleans. Do you like raw oysters?"

"I got one question for you, Carlton?"

"Okay, fire away, K. B."

"Is this oysters thing important to you?"

"Well, no, but yes, do you like raw oysters?"

"Yes, I do but is that your best come-on line?"

"Okay, K. B., I surrender."

"Just a bit of deposition, Carlton. Whatcha got in mind?"

"A place called Pascal Manale's but we can leave that question open for now."

"Nolo contendere, counselor," K. B. teased, "bye for now."

"Never expected easy. Bye."

CHAPTER 14

MAX BECKER CALLS
ALEX BONDURANT

Marcella Winslow, Executive Assistant, to Alex Bondurant had an earned a reputation as the epitome of organization and efficiency. Marcella had been with Biotherm over twelve years; the last seven as personal assistant to President Bondurant. As a matter of custom and respect, all communication to the President filtered through Marcella. This custom did not find ready acceptance amongst Biotherm employees rank or file. It was well known that any document lacking her M.W. stamp would not be seen by Alex.

An outside call rang on Marcella's desk. Her established habit was to allow at least, three rings before answering. Established habits like Marcella's are usually unappreciated by fellow workers. In actual fact, more often resentment results. Alex Bondurant was oblivious to her habits and manners. His modus operandi tended more toward a "don't rock the boat" style unless, of course, he was unaccountable for any downside risks.

She buzzed Alex and advised, "Alex, Max Becker, is asking if you are available."

"Absolutely, Marcella, I'll pick up the line in just a few seconds."

Alex hypothesized that if he answered his calls too early, callers might assume he was not as busy as he preferred them to believe.

"Max! Appreciate the call. I have been thinking that time may be overdue and lots of reasons dictate we should get together, huh? How long has it been since you and I had a dinner together at Maurice's?

"Longer than I can remember, Alex but I have an idea that might be worth considering."

"Well, Max, I do think of you as an old friend, competitive in business matters but a good, old friend nevertheless."

"Same here Alex. You want to' hear my idea?'

"Of course and absolutely, Max. I have learned sometimes at my own expense that when it comes to creative ideas, you have no equal. So, Yes, I'm eager to hear what is on your mind."

"You flatter me, Alex. First, you old coon ass, how many years did you live in New Orleans.?"

"Too many years ago for me to remember actually but as a young man, I lived there the first twenty-three years of my life; graduated from Tulane; not one of those East Coast, Yankee factories like you, Max."

My idea this time is not apt to make either of us any money. I want to suggest we meet in New Orleans during the Bio-Instrumentation meeting?"

"No, Max. Good idea, but there are two sound reasons we need to meet well before the New Orleans show."

"Tell me one." Max was using his best ol' buddy voice and clenching his teeth simultaneously.

"First one is simple Max, my young friend. You are, if memory serves me, almost twenty-five or twenty-six years younger than I am. Am I correct"?

"I'll give you a yes and a no. Stamina is a far better factor than years. Alex, it has not been all that many years, we played racquetball and you trounced me with your killer low wall smash."

"Oh my, maybe you are older than I thought. I remember that game and it was, at least, fifteen or sixteen years ago. Wait! It was precisely nineteen years, my fifty-fourth birthday."

"Alright, so what is your next excuse?"

"Call it my excuse, but I am about to tell you some very private and confidential as well as personal information."

"Alex, don't try to slip in some ruse like you are allowing the EU Research Funding Group to buy significant shares of some new offering. You can save that absurd idea for someone other than me."

"I said it was personal, didn't I? Max, I have been having chest pain attacks since last December. Angina, my cardiologist tells me is not a good indication for a man of my age. And without going into the list of diagnoses, that is not my only malady."

"I'm sorry to hear this Alex. I apologize for the foolish teasing."

"I'd like to meet with you next week at dinner. I know you enjoy Maurice's."

"Just say the time and date, Alex. I will resolve any conflicts."

"Is Wednesday evening good for you?

"You know Max between you and me we have some clout at Maurice's and if I explained to Maurice just how much you and I enjoy his Etouffee, just maybe he will prepare it especially for us Wednesday. Maurice, a typical Frenchman, is so enamored with his own culinary genius as a would be Iron Chef that he will not put great dishes on the menu. Like Etouffee is strictly reserved for dignitaries or other chefs.

"It is no secret that all kinds of configurations have been imagined regarding some cooperative venture between Gigatrax and Biotherm. Alex, any premature agreement between us must be a very private discussion. You know that insider trading is a fast route to a prison term. Too, Alex, Biotherm patents for any other company in your technology would be cherry picking. Stockholders of either company are always salivating for more and more ROI, correct?"

"That is the truth. Stockholders do expect --- no, demand bottom line rewards and it is the rare and unusual stockholder who genuinely feels the stress of operating a high tech company and constantly controlling expense in order to improve that bottom line. You know, Max, that pressure is the fuel that keeps guys like me and you running full speed."

"Absolutely, Alex, spot on, but at some point in every life, one should enjoy the spoils. You and I can look back and see the hurt, pain, and anxiety when markets seem to bottom out. I'd really like for us to consider the financial benefits to our stockholders, to our families and to us."

"Max, I am not against some kind of high ROI venture with you and Gigatrax. The ensuing details are complex. You know that, of course."

"Alex, you and I have handled far more complex challenges time and time again. Frankly, I'll bet that you and I can conjure up a big win-win in short order over a few cold ones Wednesday. Whatcha' say?"

"Okay, big guy, I'll call up Maurice and we can enjoy his E'Touffee with a nice, French wine.

"Alex, will you bring Carlton with you. Aspects of our discussion will be critically germane to him."

"Yes, Max, of course. Consider it done. --- enjoyed your call. See you at either Escondido or Gastronomique after I talk with Maurice. I'll call you back"

"Let's make it Escondido, Alex. Okay?

"Yes, Max, I totally agree. I much prefer Escondido anyway. Great!

CHAPTER 15

ROBBERY DETECTED

Verna's intercom line flashed and she heard Dr. Azran voice.

"Verna, what is he name of our Security and Mainenance Officer in the clinic?"

"That would be Manny Gomez, Dr. Azran."

"Do you know if he is in the clinic now?"

"I have not seen him, Dr. Azran but I can find out and let you know."

"Locate him. I want him in the front conference room along with you, Dr. Neeley and Dr. Hertzmann after my announcement on the P.A. system."

"Yes sir, anything else, Dr. Azran?"

"Yes, go over to the Human Relations Office and pick up the personnel file for Gomez. If they ask any questions have them call me. Bring the file to me without any discussion of this with anyone. Am I clear?"

"Yes, sir."

Dr. Azran worked closely with all his staff and employees. His email to everyone in the Clinic was a variation from his "management by walking around" style. His short announcement over the clinic's address system sounded brusque.

"The following people will report to the front conference room precisely in five minutes. Dr. Hertzmann, Dr. Neeley, Manny Gomez and Verna Kellar."

Verna rushed into Dr. Neeley's office stuttering. "Corbin, did you hear Dr. Azran's announcement? Why is he having a meeting in the front conference room anyway?"

"Relax Verna. Your hands are shaking, you are not speaking well and let me ask, why are you so damn nervous?"

"He asked me to bring you, Dr. Hertzmann and Manny into the conference room. I'm never asked to attend meetings in the Conference room. I need to locate Manny and bring him in with all of us."

The conference room was equipped with a complete audio-visual capability and a 12-foot rectangular table with installed computer monitors every few feet. Corbin and Gunter had selected seats across the table from each other. Verna and Manny remained standing awaiting entry of Dr. Azran.

"Please take a seat," Dr. Azran said as he walked into the room. He moved around the table slowly and finally selected a chair near Verna. "May I sit here Verna?"

Verna's lips moved but no words came out.

Dr. Azran removed his glasses and placed them on the table. He tapped his index finger on the mahogany table as he spoke, "I want your complete attention to what you will hear in the next few minutes. I want your complete support and willingness to help determine how these incidents happened. Do I have your support, Verna," he pointed at her awaiting an answer.

"Yes sir, of course," Verna answered.

Dr. Azran pointed to Manny and waited for his response.

"I'm not sure what you need, Dr. Azran. I will help whatever you ask."

"And you, Corbin?"

"Yes, Dr. Azran. You have my help always."

"Gunter?"

"Of course, Dr. Azran. I can help and will help in any matter whatsoever."

"Fine, as you may have noted, I am irritated. My personal space has been violated. My personal property has been stolen and I'm mad as hell."

Corbin Neeley spoke first. "What happened?"

Gunter Hertzmann interjected. "What is missing?

"Dr. Azran," Manny Gomez stood up from his chair as he asked, "What was stolen?"

"My lab coat is missing. Some of my business cards were on the floor under my office chair and a box of my personal letterhead stationery was not where I keep it on my desk. My office had been ransacked."

Manny Gomez contorted his facial expression as if he had just bit into a sour lemon. "How about the locked narcotic cabinets, Dr. Azran?"

"I think not, however, I want each of you to survey your respective areas of responsibility and provide a list of missing items or unusual observations to Manny. And, Manny, I want you to give me a detailed report after you have personally inspected the entire facility."

Dr. Azran started toward the door. Verna called after him. "Your glasses, Dr. Azran?"

"Thank you, Verna," he nodded politely as he left the conference room.

Verna, Gunter, and Corbin convened in Corbin's office to analyze what was presented in the conference room and to evaluate comments made by Dr. Azran.

Gunter's brow was furrowed like rows in a garden. The muscles in his jaw rippled as he clenched his teeth into a mean snarl. He spoke at a pace that was near indistinguishable with German language interjections. "I do not appreciate accusations or innuendoes that I might be a thief or guilty of stealing from my employer."

"I understand," Corbin added, "the entire morning is unexplainable. Dr. Azran's attitude and behavior were totally out of character. Still, I can understand his irritation that someone in his clinic would invade his private office, rifle through his desk; take some of his private stationery ---".

"And, "Verna questioned, "Why would anyone take any of his business cards?"

"I think it best that we follow Dr. Azran's orders to check our own area for any indication or forced entry or disruption of our private materials in the office." Gunter pointed to Verna and then pointed to Corbin.

Verna's pained expression validated her genuine concern. "I'd like to suggest that it may be best for me to consolidate our reports before just turning individual memos to Manny."

"--- couldn't agree more Verna," Corbin said.

"Yes, me too." Gunter chimed in. "I'm on my way back to my desk to begin."

Alone with Verna, Corbin held her hand and asked, "If you know anything about all this, it is in our best interest to share information. Do you agree on that Verna?"

"I agree but I know nothing even remotely related to the things Dr. Azran described. It probably has nothing to do with anything related but did you happen to see a well-dressed man walking across the street on a number of days. I didn't really pay much attention but as I think about it, it might have been someone surveying the Clinic building."

"I don't think there is any relationship Verna. Getting into the building would be difficult and then, Dr. Azran's office is locked whenever he is not here."

"You are probably right Corbin. I think I will put this into my section of our report anyway."

CHAPTER 16

CDC DETECTS SUSPICIOUS COMMUNIQUES

Verna Kellar rushed into Dr. Azran's office. "Sorry for not knocking, Dr. Azran. This seemed to me to be very important and I wanted to make sure you got this e-mail."

"Come on in Verna and have a seat. What do you have there in your hand?"

"I printed this email out after reading it and wanted you to see it immediately"

Dr. Azran walked around his desk and took the print out. "Thank you, Verna. Go ahead and sit down while I read this."

> *Dr. Azran: I am returning the letter we received from your research facility. The requests are patently and scientifically absurd. I have no recollection of meeting you. In fact, I did not attend the American College of Epidemiology meeting. I have read your scientific publications over the last ten or so years. However, which led me to contact the F.B.I. to further investigate. Interstate shipment of highly virulent bio-organisms is a request that I realize could not have been made by you.*
>
> *CDC has been informed by the F.B. I. that they will contact you directly to investigate this incident and take any legal actions as necessary.*
>
> *Elaine Boynton, M.D., Ph.D., Sc.D.*
> *100 Clifton Road*
> *Atlanta, GA 30333*

After a rapid scan, Dr. Azran said, "Verna, please go to the mail room and see if there is a letter or any communication from the Communicable Disease Center in Atlanta and if not advise the mail room clerk to be alert for it. I want it immediately upon arrival."

Dr. Azran was mystified by the letter from Dr. Boynton. His reputation in human epidemiology worldwide could be irreparably damaged. In actuality, even such a vicious rumor could erase years of genuine scientific integrity.

Announcements on the building P.A. system by Dr. Azran were rare. This announcement alerted Drs. Neeley and Hertzmann to come to his office immediately. The result was effective. Corbin and Gunter were both standing front and center waiting to learn the significance of the announcement.

"Sit down, gentlemen. We have a matter of utmost concern and significance. I want your undivided attention, focus, and concentration to what I'm going to describe." Again, Dr. Azran instructed them, "Sit down, please."

He recited a verbal abstract which was his interpretation of the email. Quizzical expressions from both Corbin and Gunter made it apparent to Dr. Azran that a far better explanation was warranted. He had Verna make copies of the email from Dr. Boynton and brought them to his office.

After reading the communication from the Atlanta CDC, all three men stared at each other without speaking.

Dr. Hertzmann broke the silence, "What is the significance of such a document?"

Dr. Neeley spoke next, "Documents such as this are important and highly significant. If any person or any organization might benefit or think they might benefit by such an attack --- well, false or not, the damage can be very real."

Dr. Azran held up his hand before speaking. "Have either of you heard any such rumors or even other damaging remarks?"

Corbin and Gunter looked at each other both shaking their head implying a negative. "I have a suggestion Dr. Azran, "This is a significant situation and I think a direct call from you to Dr. Boynton may be the best action that can be taken."

Dr. Azran instructed Corbin to write a response to Dr. Boynton in Atlanta and another letter to Communicable Disease Center in Australia.

"Of course, Dr. Azran." Corbin turned to Gunter asking, "Gunter, I think the response would be better if both of us cosigned with Dr. Azran. Do you agree?"

"I agree and if you will compose the letter, I will cosign as you have suggested."

Corbin stopped at Verna's desk before heading back to his office.

"Verna," Corbin spoke, "come into my office, please."

"Why in your office? How can you do the exam with no pelvic exam table?"

"We need to schedule the implant removal and it should not be done here and I do not want Gunter stumbling into the room. My surgical suite downtown is private and a better choice."

"Whatever. I'll be there in just a minute."

Once in Corbin's office, Verna asked, "Now, Corbin, what is it you want to talk about?"

"First, Verna," Corbin said "the communication from Atlanta which you read is quite important." Corbin placed his hand on Vern's knee.

"Am I talking with Dr. Neeley or Corbin? In any case, any physical exam will be done in the Exam room and sure as hell, not in your private office. So, whatever was your motivation, just get it off your mind."

"The explant is a surgical procedure, Verna. I am not talking about an exam. I am talking about the removal of the audio oscillator. Do you understand this?

"I don't understand why it is necessary to go outside to your own surgical suite."

Following a light tap, the door swung open and Gunter barged in announcing, "Corbin, I'm expecting you to generate the copy that Dr. Azran requested. I reserve the right to edit your letter before I affix my signature."

"Gunter! You invade my private office unannounced and immediately make demands. My copy will be ready before the end of the day. Please close the door as you leave."

"Verna can close the door when she returns to her workstation and I will need to speak to her after she gets back to her clinic duties."

As Verna walked toward the door, she addressed Dr. Hertzmann, "I'll come to your office right now if you need my help or if you prefer you can summon me on the intercom when you are ready Dr. Hertzmann."

"I will come by your desk later, Verna, when Dr. Neeley commands less of your time." Gunter glared at Corbin flaring his nostrils.

"I'm ready when you are, doctor."

CHAPTER 17

DON'T SPIT INTO THE WIND

V erna Kellar had a well-earned reputation at Azran Clinic for punctuality. She took pride in never taking a sick day or ever leaving early on a Friday. Hours at the clinic had been eight to five, Monday through Friday for the past twelve years. Doctors and executives usually arrived between 8:30 and 9 o'clock, but all were expected to remain on duty until the last patient of the day was gone. Verna, the early bird, usually arrived fifteen minutes before eight. Her "early to arrive" competitor, Jessie, the grounds keeper and parking lot attendant rarely punched the clock before Verna. Jessie arrived one Monday morning just minutes before her. As she pulled into the parking lot, Jessie stood to wait until he recognized her. He gave her a boy scout salute with a big, toothy grin as he walked over to greet her.

"Okay, Jessie, tell me did you sleep here last night so you could beat me to work?

"No, Miss Kellar, but you tell me did you play with the Green Bay Packers before coming here?

"I never lived in Green Bay --- not even in Wisconsin, Jessie."

"You wasn't listenin'. I was meaning Vince Lombardi."

Verna scurried off mumbling, "Is he from Wisconsin? Bye, Jessie."

After entering, Verna locked the door. Then, first observation Verna made was the number of recorded telephone calls stored. All doctors and senior executives had their own private boxes. Corbin Neeley's box had overflowed after seventeen calls.

Verna took a large stack of While You Were Out notes and made a list of callers trying to reach Corbin. The most frequent calls were from three sources. The Walnut Creek police department had left six messages. The next four messages from the FDA began at nine AM Eastern Standard time. Verna counted on her fingers mouthing. "One, two three. They started calling around five AM here."

The next message came in at seven AM from some attorney making priority demands that Dr. Neeley contacts him before noon today.

Minutes after nine, Corbin entered giving Verna a thumbs up salute.

"Here are your telephone calls," she said, "I highlighted three that sounded critical or possibly more important."

"Okay, Verna," he slurred, "please hold all my calls until after lunch."

Corbin scanned the calls that had been made and arranged them by estimated length time that might be required to answer questions or listen to patients complaining about pain or just moaning about trivia. He labeled each tele-memo assigning number 1 to the police call, number 2 to the attorney who called and number 3 to the FDA. The police department responded quickly to his call.

"Walnut Creek Police Department. Sergeant Davis."

"Yes, officer, this is Dr. Neeley calling from the Azran Clinic here in Walnut Creek. I had a call from the police early this morning before I got to the hospital."

"Good, doc, it happens that I was the one who called you earlier. A person from the FDA came in a few days ago and wants to file an assault claim against you personally and against the Azran Clinic as well."

"I know the matter you are referencing officer and can explain ---."

"No need for any explanation, doctor. I talked to the young man to redirect his thinking. Don't be concerned. No explanation is necessary. Incidentally Dr. Neeley, between you and me, this kid can be a nuisance. His father, you should know, is John Covari, County District Attorney. So, he may have a little clout. Anyway thanks for the call."

Corbin crumpled the memo in his hands and began a plot that might cause Armand Covari, or whatever his name was, some grief --- maybe, a little pain. Then, he voiced his thought "well, maybe a lot more than a little pain."

Corbin pressed the button calling the front reception area. Before Verna was able to speak, Corbin snapped at her, "Verna, bring me a fresh cup of hot coffee and a glass of ice water."

Corbin picked up memo number 2 from the attorney. The note showed a 510 area code. Corbin had anticipated some store front attorney locally in Walnut Creek. He recognized the code as Oakland. He buzzed Verna. "Verna will you make this attorney call for me. I prefer it more formal and professional. The number is ---."

"I have the number. Do you want the call made right now."

"Give me twenty or thirty seconds and see if you can get him on the line, please."

After about thirty seconds Verna called. "I have Mr. Gilchrist on ---.'

"Wait a minute Verna. Have we any previous letters, messages or emails from him?

"Nothing at all!"

"I'm taking his call now."

"Mr. Gilchrist, this is Dr. Neeley returning your call from much earlier this morning. What can I do for you?"

"Well, Dr. Neeley, I'm a doctor too and it may be what I can do for you."

"Oh, yes, J.D. is Juris Doctorate, I almost forgot. So, what can you do for me?

"Armand Covari, a registered FDA agent, came in here yesterday and wants me to represent him in a medical malpractice against you. Were you aware of his intention?

"If you want to discuss this matter, I can give you the phone number for the attorney who represents Azran Clinic."

"No, no Dr. Neeley. I limit my practice to personal injury. Malpractice is out of my league. My call is strictly a courtesy heads-up. As a matter of fact, I am just avoiding interactions with Armand's father. You know he is the County DA."

"Appreciate your concern. I have patients waiting. Thank you and goodbye."

Verna entered the office with a tray. Steam was rising from the hot coffee. She added ice cubes from a small bowl to the cup of water.

"Thank you, Verna. You are being very nice to me today. Feels like old times."

"Back off, Champ, this is only round three and we are not making up and playing kissy face. Nevertheless, you have the FDA matter to resolve. Drink your coffee and I will get the FDA for you."

"Go ahead and get FDA. What was the name of the person who called?"

"He didn't use his first name. Just Mr. Jamison. I'll get him on the line for you."

The coffee got cold and there had been no contact with Mr. Jamison."

The phone rang just before Corbin was walking toward the door. He rushed back to his desk and heard Verna on the intercom. "Corbin I have Armand Covari on hold. He says that it is vital that he speaks directly to you. I think you should take his call."

"Okay, tell him you are transferring his call to the O.R. and I'm busy extracting porcupine quills from a Dachshund's face. Then, send the call to my desk here."

Corbin had the phone to his ear before the first ring finished. "What is it this time, Covari? I know that you have made every effort to cause me grief and frustration, but you are wasting your time. Your petty name calling and visits to the police just do not bother me. Your vain efforts are a waste of your time as well as mine. So, okay, what else do you have to say?"

"My intention, you arrogant bastard, is to see you unemployed and on the street. I intend to make every effort to make your life as miserable as I can. However, Neeley, I'm not satisfied yet. I want to beat your ass real good. I will meet you wherever unless you are as fem as you look."

"You little jackass, Covari. I wrestled in college and took the state championship. So, if you think you can even bruise me, give me your phone number and I will set up the challenge."

"I want to break your nose. When you are ready call me at 510-555-02789. Neeley, you are a dead man."

"Good idea to call your Daddy and have him wipe your tears and patty pat your butt."

"Just shut up, Neeley. I know where you live and I can create a lot of grief for you."

Dr. Neeley slammed the phone down missing the cradle by four or five inches.

Verna slipped into Corbin's office and heard the last of the telecom. "Corbin, you should just leave this whole thing alone. Let a week pass and you will never hear of him again."

"I am too damn irritated at this moment to even think."

"Were you actually a wrestler, a state champion?"

"Hell no, Verna. However, I can create so much pain for Covari that he will beg for mercy."

"Yes sir, but as you just recently said this is sure not an effective use of your time."

"I heard you, Verna. But, back in Officers' Candidate School, we were taught how to defend ourselves. I did some boxing and I can still remember two Judo things that I learned pretty well."

"Anyway, Corbin, what things did you learn way back then --- back in the old days?"

"Well, one was called haraigoshi, a leg throw. The other one I can't recall right now --- no, wait, I do remember, it was the namijugi-jimi. It was a choke out. I think I could still do that."

"This still is just not a good idea, Corbin. Why don't you just forget the whole thing?"

"This coffee is ice cold. Bring me another hot coffee and look in the kitchen cabinet and if you see any fresh bagels, bring me one."

"Anything else, Massa?"

"Yes, call Covari. Tell him to meet here in our back parking lot next Saturday at noon. Tell him I said to wear his armor because I intend to bruise his toady, little ass."

CHAPTER 18

FDA: SUSPICIONS OF AZRAN CLINIC

The Friday morning sun filled the empty parking lot as Verna drove in and noticed three men --- "suits" as she called them standing in front of the clinic talking with Jessie. She parked on the far side of her regular space away from the door to avoid any discussion with the three people.

As she began walking away from her car, she noticed that Jesse was pointing his finger at her and the three men were already walking toward her.

"Good morning", gentlemen, the clinic does not open until 8 o'clock. In fact, the executives, management and doctors are not available until about 9."

Three badges were flashed before her sentence was finished. "We are federal officers from Criminal Investigations Section of the Food and Drug Administration."

Speaking nervously, Verna replied, "I'm sorry but I don't know anything about that."

"I understand --- what is your name?

"Do you have a warrant or something?"

"Just your name would help."

"My name is Verna Kellar. I am the secretary and receptionist here at Azran Clinic. Can you come back later?"

"Yes, of course, Ms. Kellar. We will go have some coffee and be back here a 9 o'clock. It is imperative that we meet with all medical personnel. Very specifically," he hesitated to read from his notepad, "Dr. Azran, Dr. Hertzmann, and Dr. Neeley. Advise them that we will be here, at least, two hours. Therefore, any patients should be re-scheduled. Additionally, please, advise Dr. Neeley that we want to meet with him privately at the close of the group meeting. Both Dr. Azran and Dr. Hertzmann will be excused during a private meeting with Dr. Neeley. Advise everyone accordingly."

"Shall I advise Dr. Neeley the subject of the private meeting, sir?" Verna queried.

"No, the meeting with him is a private matter. Do you understand, Ms. Kellar?"

"Yes, I understand, sir. May I tell your name to Dr. Neeley?"

"My name isn't important. Any suggestions for some donuts and coffee? "One of my favorites is Dutch Bros. back downtown just off the North Civic Drive and North Broadway."

"Advise your management that if they opt to have their legal counsel join our meeting that is an acceptable standard for all FDA Criminal Investigations. See you at 9 o'clock."

Well before 9 o'clock, Verna had briefed Dr. Azran, Neeley and Hertzmann in rapid, machine-gun succession and they remained sitting in the conference room.

Gunter shifted in his chair and was the first to speak when Verna ended her announcement. "Verna, are we expected to sit here alone and disregard our personal responsibilities until they saunter back into the clinic?"

"I ---", Verna stammered as Dr. Azran stood up speaking as he walked to the window. "We will be patient until they return and we will be cooperative as long as they are here. Does anyone have a problem with what I have just stated?" Azran stared at Hertzmann as he spoke each word.

"Yes, Dr. Azran, as a professional and as a gentleman, it is not necessary that I be reprised about my manners or being courteous to officers of the Food and Drug Administration." Gunter tapped on the conference table with his index finger as he spoke each word.

Corbin Neeley smiled as he listened to Gunter and moved his head as if watching a ping pong game. "Thank you, Gunter, the same goes for me as well. Nevertheless, in my opinion ---."

Dr. Azran pushed his chair away as he stood. "They are with Verna now in the waiting room." He did not wait for Verna to bring them into the conference room. He swung the door open extending his hand toward the three guests at Verna's desk. "Welcome, gentlemen. I'm Dr. Azran, please come in," he said as he extended his hand.

All three officers of the FDA nodded an acknowledgment; not one extended a friendly hand.

"Dr. Azran, I am Officer Warren. For the record this day, as I speak each of your names, please loudly announce your full name and your Azran Clinic title. Understood?

All three doctors nodded in agreement.

"Good", Officer Warren continued, "Dr. Azran."

Dr. Azran was still standing and spoke. "Doctor Harman Azran --- President and Chief Executive Officer."

Officer Warren motioned with his arm for Dr. Azran to sit down. "Dr. Neeley."

"Yes, Corbin Arthur Neeley. I'm Chief gastroenterologist."

The FDA officer pointed to Corbin as he nodded and spoke again, Dr. Neeley, are you an M.D. and what is your area of specialization?

"Yes, I am an M.D. as well as a VMD licensed to practice veterinary medicine as well."

"And, your area of specialization, doctor?"

"Primarily gastroenterology but multi-specialized."

"Explain multi-specialized."

"Of course, as an electrical engineer, I am capable and licensed to treat patients both human and other animals with electromagnetic instruments and devices."

"Fine. Thank you. Now Dr. Hertzmann?"

"Ich bin ----" Warren interrupted, "No, doctor, English, please."

"Of course, Gunter Otto Hertzmann --- Orthopedics and Neurology".

Warren altered his overly officious manner as he approached each doctor and shook hands.

"Thank each of you. The two officers sitting on this side of the table from you are observers to validate the legal record made today. However, they will not actively participate in any discussion today. Thus, introductions are not warranted.

Importantly, the purpose of our discussion today is, in no way, or any intent to determine or assign association or guilt related to any violations, FDA or Federal. To clarify, our objective is to erase any suspicion or accusations communicated by other FDA-affiliated entities."

Dr. Azran eased back into his chair and breathed deeply, expanding his chest as he questioned, "Is all this related to the communication from Dr. Boynton of the Atlanta Communicable Disease Center?'

"Indeed, Dr. Azran, that is correct. Silver Springs always investigates aspects of any and all requests for or about pathological organisms. We are aware that the requests made to both Australia and Atlanta were not written by you. Dr. Boynton spoke highly of you as did a number of scientists from the Communicable Disease Center in Atlanta."

Warren thumbed through papers from his briefcase extracting three duplicates. He placed a copy in front of Azran, another in front of Neeley and one in front of Hertzmann. "The document you see there was faxed to Silver Springs from CDC Atlanta as well as from CDC Australia."

Azran grabbed at the document wrinkling it badly as he picked it up to study the copy. "This is a totally forged signature, gentlemen. The original was obviously signed by someone else. It is near childlike --- juvenile!" Azran clinched his teeth causing his masseter muscle to swell to his ear lobe.

"My next question is critically important and is directed to each of you. Pick up the document in front of you and read it carefully and analytically --- now."

Neeley responded without hesitation, "What is the question, please?"

"Okay, Dr. Neeley, did you write the original communication using Azran Clinic letterhead?"

"Hell, no", Corbin shouted.

"Dr. Hertzmann, did you perpetrate this criminal act?"

"I did not. Of course not."

"Then, Dr. Azran, if you did not create this document, who has access to your Azran Clinic letterhead?"

"The answer to your question is a mystery. I do not know how this could happen."

"Who, Dr. Azran, has easy access to your letterhead?" Warren leaned close into Azran's face punching his two front fingers at Azran's breast bone.

"This discussion is rapidly becoming an accusation Officer Warren and I resent your treating me like a common criminal." Dr. Azran stood as if to walk away.

Warren held up his hand with palm in front of Azran's forward movement. "A simple answer is all that is required, doctor."

"Agreed," Azran replied, "I apologize for my rude and abrupt behavior. However, I can answer your question I believe."

"At this point Dr. Azran, I'd like your permission as well as Dr. Neeley's and Dr. Hertzmann's to audio\video the next few minutes. This is vital to clearing any possible malfeasance at Azran Clinic."

"Acceptable to me," said Dr. Azran.

"Me too," chimed in Neeley.

"Yes, okay for me," added Gunter.

Dr. Azran stood erect behind his chair focusing on the video lens.

"Recently, that is a few weeks ago, several things led me to think my office had been violated. First, I never leave my office door open. In fact, it is locked when I am out of the office for any time. The morning I am referring to I noticed my office door was unlocked. As I sat at my desk, I saw several of my business cards on the floor under the desk. These cards are kept in my desk drawer and I am not in the habit of dropping things and not picking them up."

"Is that the extent of your explanation?" Warren probed.

"One other peculiarity I recall. My personal lab coat is missing and it is either in my office on my side chair or in the Doctors Lounge after surgeries. I searched and it was nowhere in the clinic."

Warren smiled as he shook his head in disbelief. "Did you file a police report?

"We talked about the incident ---"

Warren interrupted, "Was a police report made, doctor?"

"No."

"Has an inventory been completed? Are any drugs unaccounted for?"

"Well, yes. All drugs are locked in glass enclosures and nothing was broken or missing."

"Very good luck doctor. At this point, you, Dr. Azran and Dr. Hertzmann are excused. We have a private matter to discuss with Dr. Neeley.

Both Azran and Gunter nodded before stepping outside into the parking lot for their own private conversation.

Dr. Neeley remained seated in the same chair. However, Officer Warren stood sorting through a portfolio of reports and selecting one which he placed in front of Dr. Neeley.

"Dr. Neeley, are you aware that successive accusations of you have been received by the Food and Drug Administration in Silver Springs?"

"--- not surprised. Agent Covari no doubt?"

"I will ask the questions doctor. I expect direct answers from you. The complaint that you have failed to file as a Medical Device Manufacturer was immediately resolved. In fact, Agent Covari was chastised and schooled that veterinary devices do not come under FDA jurisdiction."

"Yes, I suggested he read the appropriate copy of the Federal Register and stop badgering me."

"This other accusation," Warren said as he handed another page to Neeley, "is of genuine concern and I need your explanation of what occurred between you and Agent Covari.

"Simple enough," Neeley breathed a short sigh, "There was no physical altercation. Admittedly, I may have been abrupt and, possibly rude."

"Agent Covari states that you were arrogant and rude, doctor, but more importantly he verbally reported to his immediate supervisor that you had hit him and pushed him to the floor."

"Pure fabrication, Officer Warren. Flat out, damn lie. No such incident happened. Nothing." Neeley gritted his teeth evidencing his wrath.

"Okay, doctor, we are simply reporting the series of communications. There are no FDA complaints being filed against you. Apologies for any discomfort caused you today. Your time today is appreciated by FDA."

Dr. Neeley accepted the last comments as his dismal. "Goodbye, I have patients waiting."

Some twenty or thirty minutes later, the FDA entourage came out into the parking lot and drove away.

CHAPTER 19

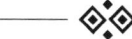

COVARI CONFRONTATION

Corbin Neeley had changed his basic, daily habits. Almost abruptly, Corbin was powering up with a dedicated vegetarian focus on nutrition and imbibing yogurts with bacterial probiotics. In the time since he had challenged Armand Covari to a street fight, he had been going to the gym for heavy weight exercises like reverse curls for his biceps. Heavy perspiration was created by interval training with short bursts of aerobic workouts. He made serious efforts to master the speed bag with miserable performance. He converted to the heavy bag until he injured his right wrist by not using proper gloves. As a means to improve his endurance, Corbin ran six laps at the nearby high school each evening.

Yesterday before his planned physical conflict with Covari, his patient load included three veterinary procedures, three geriatric colonoscopies; the first of which required laser removal of eight polyps. The third detected a suspected carcinoma that would be biopsied for validation. His concern about communicating bad news to patients took all of his energy and adversely affected his relationship with other patients. The twelve patient interactions and unusually busy telephone and email demands had pushed Corbin's to a point of exhaustion.

Today was Saturday; Corbin knew exactly what time it was. However, he had asked Verna, at least five times to tell him when it was a quarter until twelve. He was just about ready to tell her again when she walked into his office.

"Corbin, Covari, is already here in our back parking lot and you are not going to believe what you are going to see. He is wearing some kind of Ninja costume and a helmet that has horns on top. He looks like a cow of some kind. Corbin, stay inside. Don't even go out there. He is some kind of fruitcake."

"No, Verna, he is a nut of some kind but I have to make an end to his harassment." Corbin started toward the door stopping long enough to pick up a folding chair before opening the door.

"Corbin, put that chair back down and stay inside."

Corbin shook his head with a profound no and walked out facing what looked like some absurd representation of a Samurai warrior. Armand Covari shouted between growls sounding like an enraged animal. Neeley remained six or eight feet away from Covari. As he opens the folding chair, he sits down crossing his arms.

"Listen, Armand, we have taken this situation from a simple misunderstanding to embarrassing, childlike behavior. If you are willing to agree with the opinion I have just stated, we can discuss this matter and resolve it to a mutually satisfactory level."

Covari jumped with both feet leaving the ground and shot out his left leg in a clumsy attempt at a karate kick.

"Now, Neeley, is that your plea for mercy? If you will give me your full apology, I won't accept it and I will pound you even worse. Out of sheer pity, you oaf, I'll tell you what I am capable of doing to you. My sensai was Minehiko Nakano, an eighth degree, black belt who taught me jiujitsu and judo."

Neeley stood up knocking his folding chair to the ground as Covari bent forward with his head down and rushed toward Neeley yelling. Neeley used the forward momentum and Covari's own weight by stepping slightly sideways and sweeping his right leg and grabbing Covari's arm throwing him to the ground. Neeley dropped down with his knee in Covari's stomach grasping both sides of Covari's collar. Covari struggled to breath opening his mouth making gurgling and choking noises. The collar was pulled even tighter. Covari passed out completely. Neeley's aggravated emotions caused him to consider kicking Covari in the head.

"Stop! Enough, Corbin. You have killed him." Verna tugged at Neeley's arm.

"He's not dead, Verna, and he does not need your help or mine. It is over now."

"He is insane, Corbin, it is not over; believe me, please. Get back in the clinic now, please, Corbin."

Verna followed Corbin back into the clinic but, watched from the window watching for any movements. Covari showed no signs of waking. The helmet that he had worn lay next to him. Corbin waited until Verna headed back to the reception desk before stepping back outside. Fear and concern made Corbin bite his lower lip as he stepped toward Covari's silent body.

"Corbin," shouted as she came back outside, "is he breathing? Oh, my god."

Corbin has already checked for a pulse before using his stethoscope attempting to find any heart action.

"Verna, help me get him back inside and into the O.R.", Corbin pleaded.

"Is he okay, Corbin? Verna began crying.

"He has a faint and irregular heart beat. Help me get him on the surgery table --- STAT."

Verna struggled to help Corbin carry Covari inside. Corbin covered the body with a sterile sheet.

"Verna, leave the O.R. and do not allow anyone to enter. Lock the doors as you leave. Go now!"

In the later afternoon, Corbin completed all his patient commitments and was relaxing in his animal lab listening to his favorite German, Der Ring Des Niebelungen. He enjoyed the works of Richard Wagner but chose not to share this passion with Gunter. Too, Corbin exaggerated his frequency range of hearing by claiming that the actually heard 20,000 Hertz when he listens to Wagner. Some dolphins and bats might hear up to 100,000 Hz, but humans like Corbin prefer to lie about hearing such high frequencies.

He called Verna's intercom and left a message. "Verna, I'd like you to drop whatever you are doing right now and join me in the animal lab." He abruptly called with another request. "Verna, did you ever bring me the drink I asked you to get. It was either a Blood Orange Juice or a Root Beer."

"The truth is that I totally forgot that after my incident at the store and honestly I had hoped you had forgotten it as well. I apologize, Dr. Neeley and will make another trip for your soda pop if you want."

"No, of course not, Verna, don't be ridiculous or for that matter being cute is not a good fit for you."

"Alright. Would you like me to bring you a cup of fresh, hot coffee?"

"Certainly, Verna and thank you."

CHAPTER 20

DECISION TO CHANGE
BOARD OF DIRECTORS

Alex Bondurant had long suffered the pains of angina and his cardiologist had long ago recommended a nutritional plan restricting beef, most dairy products, as well as prescribing nitroglycerin pills as a near, immediate cessation of cardiac pain. In addition, the same heart doctor had advised Alex to plan an early retirement or as he put it, don't wait until your only alternative is open-heart surgery.

As President and CEO, Alex chose to believe that his angina pain was just another aspect of aging. However, for weeks now, he had strong feelings about the weakness within his board of directors. Each night, his angina kept him awake and his anxiety about Clarence Harwood added to the pain.

Alex had expressed his antagonism, fear, and frustration regarding a board member too closely affiliated with Gigatrax. It was and is factual that Max Becker, the CEO at Gigatrax, was a long time friend. Alex knew full well that such friends can be threatening when big money looks good to an aggressive, all-out war between two competitors.

Alex held controlling equity in Biotherm and, if needed, most board members would vote for most any position strongly recommended by him as Chairman --- or, for that matter as dictated as President and CEO of Biotherm.

After hours of lost sleep last night, Alex made his decision to remove Clarence Harwood from the Board of Directors. He had given serious thought to making contact with as many stockholders as reasonably possible. He knew proxy companies who could have Clarence voted out by stockholders.

He knew that proxy recommendations are most always accepted whatever recommendations are suggested. Anyone who knew Alex Bondurant knew that he never took shortcuts or looked for the easy way around any problem. His closest friends describe him as a big fullback football player who always rips through the defensive line, rarely ever goes end around or tries the long pass. Enemies that learn or know Alex's reputation will usually opt to avoid any form of competition.

Alex was in the office on time as expected and had pulled up a folding chair adjacent to Marcella Winslow's desk. Marcella scurried down the corridor toward her desk and stopped abruptly when she noticed Alex sitting there waiting for her.

"Oh, Mr. Bondurant, I'm sorry to have kept you waiting. The manager of Human Relations called me at home last night asking me to meet her in her office in the morning. She wanted to talk about some problems she has with one of our newer employees."

"That's fine, Marcella. Is it something I need to know about?

Marcella smiled as she spoke, "No, she just wanted an opinion, and, by the way, Good Morning, Boss. Do you need something on this early morning?"

"Marcella, how do you always seem to know when I am having concerns. I do need your help in contacting the Board members as follows Kenneth Elwood, Jim Caulder, Mary Ethel Harrigan and James DeVue --- and, don't forget he is the third of the DeVues."

"Of course, Alex, how would I ever forget that; He always refers to himself as James DeVue, the third. Pardon me for interrupting you."

"Please set up an Executive Board meeting three weeks from this Friday in a private room at the Sea in Palo Alto. The Executive Board will meet at three o'clock. Too, take care of arrangements for dinner; a fixed dinner menu will be good. Oh, never mind. You just take care of the details like always."

"Excuse me, sir, that will be dinner for five, correct?"

"I have always liked your acute sense of observation, Marcella. Yes, dinner for five is correct."

"Should Mr. Harwood be copied or informed of any of these matters?"

"I'm sure you made note of my saying it was to be an Executive Board meeting."

"Yes, sir! And, of course, I will detail all your instructions for your approval before any action is taken."

"And, Marcella, copy Hale Irvin. Please call him and advise him that I do want to talk with him well before this planned Executive Board meeting."

Alex began an outline of his objectives for the Executive Board meeting. He was meticulous for crafting, hardcore objectives that were always tangible, measurable and definitive. Alex used this method which he called objective, strategy, and methods. He demanded all executives and departmental managers to develop this skill and execute beyond any vague, blue sky targets that were unmeasurable and lacking objectivity. The management style was shared between all departments of the company which permitted every employee to see and measure results. Each objective was target-dated and attached to a clearly communicated strategy which demonstrated the logic and means to achieve the objective. Any potential objective remained in review until finely detailed methods clarified the chronology from beginning to completion. Alex was reviewing the details of his favorite management system; an alert light on his intercom caught his attention.

"Yes, Marcella, am I missing an appointment. We were just talking a minute or so ago." Alex made the remark with a muffled, tongue-in-cheek style.

"Alex, that was about eight-thirty almost an hour ago. Anyway, sir, I have Mr. Irving holding for you."

"Good, Marcella, I'll take his call now, please," he said, "Hale, appreciate your call. I need to discuss a situation that has been agonizing me for all too long and I want you to check your calendar and be able to sit in and preside over an Executive Board meeting."

"Of course, Alex. Marcella gave me the basics including time and place. The Sea is a great dinner house. How did you happen to pick it."

"I totally agree. However, meeting rooms there are quiet and isolated from all outside sounds."

"Sounds okay to me as long as someone from The Palo Alto Times will not be sitting in."

"We should discuss Clarence Harwood's termination specifically regarding potential legalities; Clarence has a substantial amount of equity non-vested ---".

"No real concern, Alex. I will review the Biotherm Articles of Incorporation and analyze Clarence Harwood's employment agreement as well as make a judgment on how litigious he tends to be. For the time, Alex, such worries are not the best use of your time. Relax --- go fishing, take a day off. I'll call you with a firm plan of attack in a day or so."

"Sure, Hale. I haven't been fishing, at least, can't remember it. Appreciate your call. Talk later!"

"One more minute, Hale. There are further organizational changes

DIABOLIC SOUNDS OF SILICON VALLEY

pending consideration. If you can expedite any aggravations related to this Clarence Harwood matter. It will be appreciated. Too, some early --- in fact, very early discussions have been initiated which would or might demand an entirely new Board of Directors. As these thoughts come to fruition, I will, of course, keep you integrally involved. Enjoyed our talk today, Hale."

"Same here, Alex, and I was serious about taking some time off. Go fishing whatever. Call you later."

CHAPTER 21

K. B. FLIES WITH CARLTON

B iotherm and Gigatrax had both reviewed all the ramifications of the
meeting of the Bio-Instrumentation Academy in New Orleans. An
engineer statistician had completed a Gantt chart for the meeting objectives
in detail.

K. B. and Carlton had their own plans to attend the conference in New
Orleans. These plans included flying together with prospects for a dinner
meeting to be established after arrival in New Orleans.

Carlton had specific details including flying American Airlines, Boeing
737-900, first-class seats 3A and 3B which were convertible to full-length
beds. He had arranged for limousine shuttles to pick them both up for an
8 AM flight to New Orleans as well as pick up when they returned to San
Francisco. Privately, he had set up dinner reservations for Pascal Manale, his
favorite place to eat in New Orleans --- well outside of the Quarter.

Carlton had negotiated for two, first-class seats, 3A and 3B, on a newly
released Boeing 737-900. His long-time membership in the American Airline's
Admirals' Club provided him enough clout to get the two, first-class seats at
a substantially reduced price. These seats were convertible to full-length
beds but would offer no benefits on the short flight between SFO and New
Orleans. Carlton's twisted logic was that such comfortable potential would
provide for more provocative conversation during the flight.

On takeoff, K. B. and Carlton felt the gravity forces generated by the
737 rapidly gaining altitude as they enjoyed the heavily padded backs of their
cushy, first-class seats. They both had requested Champagne cocktails when
they first boarded. The intended altitude was reached in record time and they
were ordering their second drinks.

"Well, Carlton, my seatmate and newest friend," K. B. said as she leaned toward Carlton, "your bottom line at Biotherm must be nice."

"K. B., why don't we make a pact for the next few days, okay?" Carlton nodded his head as he smiled.

"Sure, but my remark was not about financials, Carlton. I was just wondering if you always fly first-class."

"No, unless I get bumped up from the back row, cheap seats or have enough flight credits and never as classy as these seats."

"Carlton, I was not oblivious. These seats are full sized beds and probably beautiful on international flights."

"You did notice, huh?, Carlton asked, "my million miles --- probably, well over a million on American allows me a few special privileges."

"You are not about to hear a single complaint from me, Carlton, I'm going to enjoy every day of this trip."

"As will I, K. B.", he said, "I have always liked New Orleans, the great restaurants, French/Creole foods, seafood of unusual varieties as well as some of the entertainment along Bourbon Street."

"What was the thing that you mentioned before I interrupted you?'

"No biggie, K. B. --- ah, I was going to suggest that we keep business conversation to a minimum and just relax and enjoy some fun times together --- if you feel comfortable with that."

"Almost agree, Carlton. I genuinely want to get to know you better. Your reputation precedes you in Silicon Valley."

"So, do you want to hear the derogatory stories about Carlton Herrick or the phony, embellished stories of my big sales successes or my other personal conquests."

"I promise not to pry or attempt to delve into your foibles, business or personal. After all, Carlton, you do have a kind of big man on campus reputation in medical product sales and marketing."

"Frankly, K. B., there is no way I can even hold a candle to your undergrad degree GPA. In fact, your J.D. and experience as a D.A. make me look like a kindergartner getting a sticky, smiling label on his report card."

"Come now, Carlton, your path to the vice-presidency is an almost unbelievable story."

Carlton laughed abruptly spilling his drink onto his shirt. K.B. picked up a napkin from her tray and dabbed at the wetness from the spill.

Carlton impulsively grabbed her hand holding the cloth napkin.

"Oh, I'm sorry, Carlton. I feel responsible for spilling the drink on your shirt."

"My own fault, clearly I get a little nervous talking to you. Anyway, I have more shirts packed."

K. B. had continued holding the cloth napkins to absorb any remaining wetness. She realized she was still rubbing at his shirt. "Sorry about the accident. Do you want another drink?"

"Yes but you know, I was getting used to your attention," he said, "and beginning to like it."

They both snickered and buzzed the stewardess for one more bottle of Champagne.

"By the way, K. B., thank you for your concern and for your help mopping up the Champagne that I so clumsily spilled," Carlton commented as he patted her hand.

"Call it 'the milk of human kindness' if you insist on patting my butt over an insignificant happenstance."

"Yes, K. B., I never drink milk" Carlton stuttered, "but your butt does open some creative thinking."

"Ah, a little lechery is indicated by your little bit of stuttering. Are you feeling lecherous, Carlton, or what?"

"I can't answer that and I wasn't patting your butt even though I did give that some thought and, having said that, before the stewardess returns, would you like to try the feel of these full-length beds?"

"Oh, my, Carlton, your audacious reputation comes to the forefront. So, what are you suggesting anyway?"

"Hold on, K. B., audacious innuendoes are not my style. I apologize for my lack of clarification or whatever I said that caused you to misunderstand."

"No misinterpretation on my part, Carlton. Frankly, your invitation did arouse my interest."

"You know, K. B., I'm glad we decided to fly together. We seem to communicate easily together." Carlton smiled.

"Me, too, Carlton, day in day out talking business, legalities, financial ramifications and calculating the same old, threadbare income statements just are not stimulating to me anymore," K. B. chatted, "so, my senior executive, how about you?"

"Well, K. B.," Carlton agreed, "I can absolutely understand your thinking. In my case, following years in field sales and nursemaiding new sales hires, my exec responsibilities are welcome changes."

"It may surprise you, Carlton," K. B. said, "that if I were to do it all over, I would have really enjoyed reporting to a man like you."

"Wow! Indeed!" Carlton responded with a smile ear to ear, "However, you surely have observed that I can't keep my eyes from surveying your beauty, your face --- your body and ---."

"And, Carlton, it should not surprise you that I enjoy every glance you make, I have noticed that you do not breathe any harder as you look over my body from top to bottom." K. B. teased.

"You know, K. B., you do not see everything. Why did I spill the champagne?"

"I'm not sure, Carlton. So, let's share another bottle. What do you think?"

"K. B., I think my mind and my imagination are running rampant. Good that you can't read my mind."

"Then, again, Carlton, I might get some excitement from reading your mind."

CHAPTER 22

OYSTERS AT PASCAL MANALES

Carlton and K. B. had explored all the usual tourist attraction in the French Quarter of New Orleans. Bourbon St. begins at Canal St. and extends thirteen blocks from Canal Street to Esplanade Avenue. Both sides of Bourbon Street were chockablock full of shops jammed one following the next. They had walked into several restaurants, three souvenir shops, a praline candy manufacturer, listened to dixie-land jazz in a bar as well as another trio of musicians playing on the street and passed right by the red beans and rice store. She experienced a friendly imposition by a young black man telling them her how much he liked her shoes and that could tell her where she got them as well as what size they were.

Carlton put his hand on the small of her back and gave her an easy tug saying, "Young man, we already been there, done that. You need a new gimmick." Pulling K. B. a bit closer, he encouraged her," Come on. We got lots of things to see and do."

K. B. slowed and dropped a few steps behind Carlton as she chided him, "You needn't be rude or so crass." Carlton observed her staring at a well-illuminated sign reading Marie Laveau's House of Voodoo.

K. B. shook her head right and left in disbelief. It may have been fear. It could have been disgust. She had previously read books about voodoo and knew that Marie Laveau had reportedly died in 1881.

Carlton placed his hand on the small of her back again and asked, "Do you want to step inside and take a look?"

"Yes, I really do. This kind of culture is fascinating to me."

"Come on, counselor. Are you putting me on"? Carlton smiled and winked at her.

"No, Carlton, I have read voodoo explanations from scientists from the nineteenth century and the psychology of such practices taken from Africa have a certain amount of credibility --- no, really." She returned his smirky grin.

K. B. seemed intrigued with the vast assortment of voodoo masks. She held up each one getting up to Carlton's face with two or three spooky sounds. She followed that with, "Scared you, huh?"

Carlton put his arm around her shoulders as he leaned close enough to whisper in her ear. "Are you thirsty?" Ready for a real New Orleans drink?'

"Maybe, yes and maybe, no. And, by the way, are you called anything besides Carlton?"

"Well, K. B., yes, of course. Are you called anything other than K. B.?

"You tell me yours and I'll tell you mine later." This remark came with a twitch of her nose. "Okay, another a small drink might be good, "she said.

K. B. selected another voodoo mask and after holding up to her face and checking her appearance in the mirror, she pulled the elastic band over her head and looked again into the mirror. She opened the top of her blouse by loosening three top buttons and folding each side underneath exposing a glimpse of suntanned breasts. Turning to Carlton with her hands behind her head she walked toward him whispering, "I like this one. You know what? I think I could get into this voodoo thing down here in Naw'lins. What do you think? Do you like the way I look?"

"You look like a morsel of some kind. I do like the look it gives you as well as the feeling it gives me."

"Where can we go to get that New Orleans drink you talked about --- if you are ready." With that, she took off the mask and put it down on the other display masks. With a little sigh, she asked, "You ready for the drink?"

"More than ready, but I have to pay for something first. I bought you a New Orleans juju."

"What? Let me see what. What is it?

"Not right now. Later!" Carlton took her arm and pulled her closer.

On the other side of Bourbon Street about a block away, they walked close together toward Pat O'Brien's.

K. B. giggled, "Now, I see where we are headed and I bet even money you plan on buying me a Hurricane and assume the rum will make me more attentive."

"Huh –uh, K. B. --- are you getting a little hungry?

"For Red Beans and Rice? Nope, not hungry at all."

"That's what I thought, K. B. and after the Hurricane, we can grab a cab and head Uptown for Pascal Manale's."

"I'm guessing that may be one of your favorite restaurants. Am I correct?"

"Absolutely, K. B., the seafood there is always fresh and unusually prepared."

K. B. hesitated then slowly stuttered. "Well, in that case. I am getting hungry. I'm ready --- if you are."

Back on Bourbon Street, cabs are readily available. Carlton held the door for her and slid in next to her as he placed his hand close to her leg.

"Carlton, are you staying at the Marriott?"

"No, I have a room in the French Quarter on Conti Street."

"That surprises me. The French Quarter is so noisy. Why do you like the place on Conti?"

"The main reason is that it is a matter of habit. Actually, Conti is in the Quarter --- no question, but there is never the noise or the hubbub like Marriott's. Too, I have a policy of avoiding drinking or partying with all the salespeople here at the show. In fact, if I have a drink, I really prefer my solitude."

"That surprises me even more. However, I do agree with your rationale. My personal choices are somewhat like your thinking. I never join other Gigatrax executives for drinks or, for that matter, fraternization with field salespeople is always a bad idea."

"I can understand your thinking, okay, but you do know that I was one of those sales people that you now avoid."

K. B. grabbed his hand and squeezed it gently as she whispered, "Yes, I know that. In fact, I know far more about you than you might know. However, tonight is different. It isn't a business. This is a friendly date, okay?"

Pascal Manale's was far enough away from the French Quarter and was not crowded like the Quarter.

"As a starter on our first date, we should have a real New Orleans drink --- it is called a Sazerac with the flavor of anise and a touch of absinthe," Carlton pontificated. "I hope Eddie Boudreaux is still bartending here; he makes an old fashioned, Old Fashion," Carlton said repeating himself, "and really muddles the orange slice and the cherries to a perfect result. I was first sent here from downtown a few years ago; the bartender at Marriott's told me to go here and ask for Boudreaux because, as he put it, he couldn't compete with Eddie on the Sazerac."

"And, so, Carlton, what is your recommendation. Better yet, you order and just surprise me."

"You like surprises, huh? Alright, we will pass on both Old Fashions and Sazeracs for something, I hope, you will enjoy."

K. B. leaned into Carlton touching his chin with her finger as she gave him a breathy response, "I'm up for most anything tonight. So, what is this that I will remember for a long time?"

"First, I will order two, cold beers for us and pay for the oysters we are going to have shortly."

"Why do you have to pay for the oysters here at the bar, Carlton? The oyster bar is over in a corner. I noticed it when we came in."

The bartender provided the beers and oyster tickets that Carlton had ordered. They headed to the oyster bar where Carlton taught her how to prepare a paper cup of catsup, fresh horseradish, Worcestershire sauce, some black pepper, and a dash of Tabasco.

Cold, fresh oysters were being shucked and set on the oyster counter between Carlton and K. B. faster than either of them could eat them.

After quite a few oysters had disappeared, K. B. said, "Before another single drink, Carlton, I want to tell you how much I have enjoyed these last two days with you. A mutual friend, that is, a close girlfriend of mine told me about you when I told her we were flying together to New Orleans."

"And, my little, tipsy friend, what did your friend say about me?"

"She said that you were a man's man and a gentleman's gentleman and now, I understand her remark. Today has been fantastic. I appreciate your being with me because I know you had lots of business demands that you postponed."

"Don't believe everything you hear about me, K. B. --- most stories like those I make up myself. Well, anyway, I want to say something too. These two days have been mentally stimulating to me and I enjoy your company immensely."

"My goodness, Carlton, have we had too much alcohol today. Did you say mentally stimulating? I was wishing you might feel a little physical stimulation." She pulled him close as she spoke and kissed him on the cheek.

"How many oysters did you eat, K. B." Carlton teased.

K. B. laughed. "I don't know. Who counts?

Somehow, even the idea of dinner had evaporated like the oysters had disappeared.

The complimentary conversation continued on the cab ride back downtown.

K. B. spoke. "Will you drop me off at the Marriott?"

"Of course, remember I am a gentleman unless you would like to see my hotel on Conti."

"I'd prefer to see your hotel on Conti. Can we stop off there first?"

The French Quarter was bustling with people and the bars were still packing in the drinkers. As Carlton had described, his hotel was as silent as a monastery. The noise from Bourbon Street was magically gone as they walked through the lobby.

Carlton walked behind K. B. and as she stopped to look at a painting, He placed his hands around her waist.

"Carlton," she said, "you told me earlier that you were mentally stimulated ---.

"K. B. ---," he hesitated. You are physically exciting to me --- very much, in fact."

She turned facing him pressing her body to his. "I knew that when we were coming back in the cab."

"The bar is still open, I'd guess. I know the bartender. Would you like a nightcap?'

"No, not tonight."

"That is fine with me as well. By the way, I have a gift for you that feels most appropriate right now."

"What did you buy, Carlton. I saw you pay at the voodoo shop as we were leaving."

"It is just a simple talisman as something for you to remember our fun times in New Orleans."

K. B. put the talisman in the palm of her hand. "I love it. Thank you", she said.

"In New Orleans, such a talisman is called a juju. It should bring you luck and good fortune."

"Thank you," she said.

"Would you like to see my room while we are here, K. B.?"

"Sure, so, let's go to your room."

Carlton remembered something from his selling days: Don't continue closing when you already have the order.

CHAPTER 23

ANGINA: ALEX BONDURANT

Marcella Winslow arrived at the Biotherm complex feeling a bit unnerved. An unreliable wi-fi alarm system had failed to get her up and her day was starting late before it even got started. She finished her morning toilet, dressed hurriedly and began an email to her office. After a deliberate thought, she decided that the email communication wasted her effort this morning. Her established habit of always being to work early was in jeopardy which added to her anxiety and apprehensiveness.

"Shoot!", she shouted as she tore the sleeve of her blouse, "what is happening next?"

Of all mornings, her aging Volvo barked back at her and showed few signs of starting. She removed the keys, got out of the car, and managed to lift the hood of the Volvo. Knowing effectively nothing about internal combustion, engines, motors or, for that matter, nothing whatsoever about electricity, she looked under the hood and shouted again, "Stupid machine!" After kicking the side of the front door, she concluded that her only remaining option was to try the same things again like starting the car. The result met her every expectation. She would be a few minutes late, but she felt she might be at her desk before Mr. Bondurant arrived. She hypothesized that he might be a little later himself today.

Marcella tossed her purse in the drawer of her desk. Then, she scurried into Mr. Bondurant's office to explain her tardiness this morning. The office was empty and no signs of him having been here earlier.

Back at her desk, she noticed the blinking LED lights on her desk fax. She grabbed the printout and scanned it quickly. It read:

Marcella\ My angina even with my nitroglycerin pills passed the tolerable threshold last night beyond my control. Ambulance to El Camino Hospital; transferred to Stanford Hospital in Palo Alto. They claim I'm here for short-term observation.

There really is no genuine reason for concern. I will be back on the job in a day or so.

Please maintain my communication privately. Minor nose sniffles from me can drive the market down --- sorry for my poor sense of humor.

I do think it advisable to advise Carlton --- not a warning. He is at the Bio-Instrumentation meeting in New Orleans. That is more important than having him fly back.

For inquiries, say that I am taking a few days of relaxation in Tahoe.

Marcella had the itinerary provided by Carlton which clearly described his day to day activity plan with appropriate telephone numbers for every location. She contacted his hotel on Conti St. leaving him a private message to call her. No details were provided. Within the next hour, she called Carlton's cell number again leaving the message to call her whenever possible.

As it happened, "whenever possible" did not sound like an emergency. From the perspective of anyone awaiting a call that had been specifically requested, any delay in response feels like eternity.

Marcella, of course, could not have imagined why Carlton had not returned her requested call immediately. In her mind, the angina discomfort Alex was suffering was the highest priority. For a subordinate executive to not return an urgent call was not even close to her imagination.

Marcella considered reporting Carlton's insubordination directly to Alex. However, the risk of personal repercussion blocked any activity other has simply waiting until Carlton called.

CHAPTER 24

CARLTON VISITS AZRAN CLINIC

Carlton left his office in Palo Alto heading directly across the Bay north up 580 toward Walnut Creek. His intent was to call Verna and set up a meeting with Dr. Azran. It was just past morning traffic and the roads were clear. He opened his communication system by voicing "Alexa, call Azran Clinic in Walnut Creek.

The voice responding sounded like Verna to him as she spoke, "Good Morning, Azran Clinic."

"Hi, Verna, I had some responsibilities in the East Bay today and I have two requests. First, are you available for lunch when I get to Walnut Creek?'

"Probably, Mr. Herrick, ask me when you get here, okay?'

"This is Carlton unless you are upset with me for whatever."

"Of course not Carlton and I can arrange for you to meet Dr. Azran if you would like."

"Perfect plan Verna. How about when we are back from lunch?"

"I'll do my best unless he has previous commitments."

"Okay, that is good enough for me. See you within the next hour or so. I'll call when I'm close."

"Goodbye and thank you for your call as well as the lunch invitation."

As Carlton considered the traffic ahead, he smiled to himself thinking about how many times he had made this same trip just to survey the comings and goings of employees of the Azran clinic. He smiled even bigger as he recalled sneaking into the back entrance, dressing up like an in-house janitor and locating Azran's business cards, lab coat with the embroidered name and

M.D. title. He even chuckled under his breath when some employee asked him to do his office cleaning next. Now, he was again tracking the same route but with an invitation to meet an expert on diseases and things like that.

Asking Verna to lunch was far from happenstance. It was an element in his strategy to get an insider explanation as to what unusual things might have happened in the clinic over the last days. Carlton felt a few seconds of fear when he visualized himself sitting in front of Azran's desk with the victim staring directly at the person who ripped off his lab coat.

"Alexa, call Azran Clinic." Verna responded, "I just saw you pass by and thought you missed the turn. Come on in."

Following the streets, as he had done previously, he drove directly toward the back parking lot. He had to turn around and take the front entrance parking.

Verna was waiting outside the front door seeming to be excited to see him. Her bearing was a practiced approach greeting all incoming patients. "Good to see you again. How far did you have to drive to get here?"

"From Palo Alto, it is just a little over an hour depending, of course, on traffic or what local sporting events are jamming the freeways."

"I'm sorry Dr. Azen won't be in the clinic until this afternoon. However, I have a surprise that you will enjoy. Dr. Corbin Neeley is substituting for Dr. Azran and will give you the guided tour. Be prepared to hear more about febrile disease, gastric disorders or veterinary medicine than you ever wanted to know."

"I am already impressed. Is he a medical doc as well as a veterinarian?"

"And --- an electrical engineer with patents in thermoelectric devices applicable to disorders."

"Wow, now I am humbled."

"Well, wait and see. He will be meeting you about 1:30 - 2:00 when we are back from lunch if the invitation is still open."

"Of course, you are still invited. I'm looking forward to getting to know you and about Azran Clinic. Do you know a good place in Walnut Creek?"

"Yes, if you happen to like Portuguese beans. Tony's is a good spot."

"Well, not sure about Portuguese beans. If they are spicy, I'll probably like them. Can we go now? I'll drive if you do the navigation."

"I need a few minutes to change out of my work smock. Is it cold outside?"

"Not really cold but you might need a sweater. I noticed a cool breeze this morning."

"I do have my sweater. I'll put it on."

"Can we leave for lunch now?"

As Carlton drove out of the parking lot, he took an admiring long look at what Verna had called a sweater. The sweater had a row of buttons down the center from her neck to mid belly. He mentally questioned why four of the buttons from her neckline were obviously left open. He deliberately put those thoughts out of his mind.

Parking in downtown Walnut Grove was a challenge as well as a certain nuisance to Carlton. It seemed that Verna's idea of a good place to have lunch was not in configuration with Carlton's expectations. He recognized that this gaudy place for lunch would appeal to young people who were ecstatic with a greasy hamburger, French fries or Tony's beans. Nevertheless, he calculated the available time was limited and the noise level would make any casual conversation near impossible.

Verna pointed to a table in need of clearing. "Will you grab that table for us and I'll go put our orders in --- if you can trust my judgment."

"I'll have whatever you are having and will commandeer the table for us." Carlton looked around the crowd with an expression of derision. Under usual circumstances, he would have shaken his head in disgust and headed for the exit.

Verna returned to the table with her hands full of paper bags and two paper cups of liquid of some kind. "So, what do you think, Mr. Herrick? I hope you were not hoping for a more upscale place for lunch."

"This is great Verna. It reminds me of places I used to eat when I went to college. The hamburgers are perfect and I haven't had curly fries like this in a long time. Go ahead and eat as we talk." Carlton was realizing that he had lost sight of his primary objective of being in Walnut Creek and he was definitely not making the best use of his time.

"Oh, Carlton, I notice you are not really eating Tony's Portuguese beans. Don't you like them?"

Carlton said, "Not too bad" but he was thinking back home as a kid in Illinois, they feed this kind of stuff to the pigs.

The drive back to the clinic was mostly uncomfortable silence except for Verna's repeating her apology for her poor selection of restaurants. Carlton acted graciously and said, "I actually enjoyed the atmosphere."

As they entered the side door into a hallway that led to several private offices, a doctor clad in green pastel, surgical scrubs was walking toward them.

"Mr. Herrick, may I introduce you to Dr. Corbin Neeley, a physician/surgeon specializing in gastroenterology as well as veterinary medicine." Verna stopped talking and took a deep breath and continued speaking, "Dr. Neeley is a physicist as well with patents in treating disease with sound."

Dr. Neeley held up both hands at eye level and clapped his applause. "Mr. Herrick, you have just heard a totally embellished and exaggerated introduction. I have to say that as Verna spoke I was looking around to see who she was talking about."

"And a nice intro I'd have to say. You must have years of medical and scientific education. I guess you have earned several titles as a doctor. That is very impressive, Doctor."

"Appreciate your compliment and I am far more at ease being called Corbin --- been called far worse."

Carlton nodded and began smiling as Corbin held out his hand for a welcoming handshake. "Me, too, Corbin. I mean in my case far worse."

"Verna", Corbin mumbled, "Carlton and I will be getting to know each other as we tour the facilities here at the Azran clinic. Follow me, Carlton, and I'll tell you more about myself and what I do here day to day."

"Excellent Corbin. I may need to ask a few questions as we talk to make up for my scanty scientific background."

"Relax and don't hesitate to interrupt me if anything I describe is unclear.

First, I want to show you my personal lab which is adjacent to the dog kennels. After meeting my dogs, we can walk through the primate section which can be louder than the barking dogs at times."

"Right here is the lab. This has some of the best electronic equipment and allows me to develop new, electromagnetic devices ---"

"Ahh, Corbin. A bit more explanation about electromagnetic if you will."

"Yeah, for example, do you know what a TENS device is used for?"

"No, but I am interested."

"TENS is a mnemonic for Transcutaneous Electrical Nerve Stimulation, okay?

"Yes and no, my good doctor. Can you tell me how a TENS is used?"

"Yes, it is pretty straight forward. An injury --- for example, playing basketball, a person falls and has pain in the hand and pain in the knee. Pain is experienced in the brain but the brain has a problem sorting out multiple signals. The TENS device has numerous electrical contact points that carry a selected voltage; these points attached to the back of this patient and a small electrical shock is applied by the TENS. In fact, so many small shocks that distract from other pain like the hand and knee. Do you follow the logic of such treatment?"

"Well enough, Corbin. Good explanation. So, it is a matter of substituting a new pain to mask another."

"Good --- close enough.

"Here is the canine section. Noisy guys, aren't they. These dogs of various breeds belong to owners who brought them here for examination and treatment. Some may spend several days for observation."

"Now, that I understand."

"Do you own a dog, Carlton?"

"Yes, I do. She is a small poodle --- near miniature. I had to take her to my vet in Menlo Park."

"What was her problem? You are a veterinarian correct?"

"No, my undergraduate studies are not even close to your accomplishments."

"I see. Go ahead telling me about your poodle."

"My neighbor knocked on my door late one afternoon carrying Lilly. He explained that he had drained his antifreeze into a pan and thought she might have eaten some of it?

"What was her condition at that point, Carlton?"

"I could not see any behavior change but called the vet anyway."

"She said that antifreeze is highly toxic which I knew and told me to bring her in for overnight observation."

"Good decisions all around. You possibly saved Lilly's life. Dogs can die from drinking or eating alcohol like ethyl alcohol and antifreeze. Ethylene glycol poisoning is caused by drinking ethylene glycol like antifreeze. Early symptoms include intoxication, vomiting, and abdominal pain. Later symptoms may include a decreased level of consciousness, headache, and seizures. Long-term outcomes may include kidney failure and brain damage. The overnight observation was a sound decision."

"I picked her up the following day and she looked perfectly well."

"Early treatment increases the possibility of a good outcome. Treatment consisted of stabilizing Lilly, followed by the use of an antidote. The preferred antidote is fomepizole."

"Corbin, thanks for the valuable information. My vet didn't give me one tenth of the info you just detailed. I appreciate it very much."

"I like telling patients good stories of positive results. Incidentally, did you hear about the killing of Kim Jong Un's Brother-in-law in the Kuala Lumpur airport in Malaysia."

"Yes, it was on all the TV news in February."

"The chemical that was rubbed on his face by some girl was VX, a human-made chemical warfare --- a nerve agent. Nerve agents are the most toxic and rapidly acting of chemical warfare agents. Just 10 milligrams of the nerve agent or a single drop is enough to kill in minutes."

"Where would such a dangerous poison be available?"

"VX is like a pesticide on steroids, this is an extraordinarily toxic substance, roughly 1/100th of a gram --- just 100 milligrams, on someone's skin, will kill before the ambulance arrives. VX makes antifreeze look like a cocktail."

"That is really scary stuff. Makes you wonder if it is stored in drums or barrels in North Korea."

"That is scarier stuff, Carlton. Sorry for taking you on that terrible story. Here as we enter this door, we are in the primates area."

Following the tour and all the information provided by Dr. Neeley, Carlton spent another half hour with Verna thanking her for such an enjoyable opportunity.

Verna placed her hand on Carlton's arm speaking "I'm glad you liked the experience. I'd like to see you again sometime."

Carlton eased toward the exit door. "It could be arranged, Verna. Bye for now."

CHAPTER 25

VERNA KELLAR: OXYCODONE

Corbin was once again relaxing and listening to Der Ring Des Niebelungen and once again fabricating to himself that he could hear some of Wagner's frequencies beyond the human range of hearing. Just recently, he stubbornly tried to convince Gunter that he could easily hear the 20,000 Hz when listening to the babbling of his water feature. Gunter had paid little attention and turned his back walking away from Corbin jabbering back something unintelligible in German that probably might translate to absurd or stupid.

As the Wagner music ended, Corbin experienced a momentary pang of guilt. He prided himself with his absolute commitment to a total focus on his responsibilities as a physician and a scientist. It would only be a rare event or unusual set of circumstances that he might allow time for relaxing or casual contemplation.

With no scheduled appointments and opting to disregard his other duties, Corbin was leisurely strolling through the clinic and noticing Verna sitting in the coffee room. He pulled up a chair next to her and tried to begin a conversation.

"Alright, Corbin, go ahead and sit down. I know you want something so just go ahead and say what you were going to say." Verna used her most churlish tone.

"Not a very polite way to start our talk, huh? Contrary to your expectation, I want to do something for you."

"Corbin you know what I need and I have made it completely clear to you. I'm again warning you if you do not remove the thing you implanted in my uterus, I will report what you have done to both Gunter and Dr. Azran."

"Okay, please don't threaten me when I am doing everything, the very best I can for you. Prepare the O.R. between 4 and 5 today and meet me there. I will do whatever you want. Is that good enough for you? Will you be ready for the O.R. no later than 4 o'clock?"

"First Corbin. Have you looked at a clock or your watch or checked your telephone? Do you know what time it is at this moment? I'll tell you. It is after three o'clock approaching late afternoon. There are no patients scheduled for the O.R. today. Dr. Hertzmann has been in San Diego the last two days. Unless you are making some excuse for doing what I have asked you to do, right now is fine with me. I will wait in the O.R. while you scrub!"

"Agreed Verna. You will need some pre-op medications, nothing more than a mild tranquilizer. The whole procedure will take less than fifteen minutes --- 20 minutes at most." Corbin patted her hand.

"What tranquilizer? Any other medications?"

"Only a new little blue pill trademarked as Percoset, the ones marked 512."

"Fine, give them to me so we can get this over before five o'clock."

"They are on your desk already so take them immediately. I planned all this earlier today."

Forty-five minutes later Verna positioned herself prematurely in the Harvey stirrups device. Her pupils were reduced to pinpoints and she slurred her words as Corbin approached her.

"Corbin! What did you give me to take? I can't even see straight and I can see that you did not scrub. You are wearing the same clothes and the same the same lab coat. Damn, Corbin, what the hell is going on."

"The procedure does not require sterility and as I said earlier, it will take maybe fifteen minutes. So, get comfortable in the stirrups and slide down toward me just a bit. Okay, that's good."

"Corbin, this was not what was supposed to happen and I want you to stop now. I'm afraid, Corbin. Please, help me get up. I need to sit up. Dr. Hertzmann came back to the clinic about an hour ago. I want him in here." Her last words trailed off as Verna slipped deeper under the influence of the opioid.

The automatic doors to the smaller O.R. opened creating an alarm that signaled a potential violation of sterility. Gunter literally barreled into the room pushing Corbin when he saw Verna sprawled in a lithotomy position, typical for gynecological examination or surgical purpose.

Corbin screamed at Gunter, "You stupid kraut, Gunter." Corbin swung wildly missing Gunter's face and again falling to the floor and shouting, "Gunter, you bastard, I'll kill you, you son of a bitch". Corbin attempted to get to his feet and Gunter hit him with a strong right cross dropping him once again to the floor.

Gunter's voice had the growl of an enraged animal. "Kill me will you, Corbin. If you get up, I will break your hands. Never ever will you be capable of even removing a splinter."

Gunter checked Verna's vital signs and detected what he felt might be a fibrillation. He called an emergency ambulance unwilling to make guesses or assume she would show improved heart sounds. Her drugged conditions were obvious to any observer with or without medical experience.

Gunter felt that some immediate action was needed to stop all of Corbin's illicit and illegal actions. His attempts to reach Dr. Azran on the O.R. intercom failed. In his confusion, he recalled that Dr. Azran was over at the University of California in Berkely today attending a presentation on new outbreaks of E. coli.

Gunter's anger was driving him to contact either the FDA or the Drug Enforcement Agency. His hesitation was solely due to not being able to involve Dr. Azran.

The Ambulance siren announced the arrival of emergency paramedics. Four of them were already attending Verna. Gunter stood in the outer ring of the paramedics and was able to see the label on a vial of Narcan. He knew that naloxone is commonly an antidote for opioids like heroin, morphine, oxycodone, and Vicodin. Gunter fully understood that overdosing on an opioid can slow down or stop breathing. He knew, as well, that a victim of an opioid can be very hard to revive.

During all the time, heart rate and oxygen transmission were constantly monitored. At one point, Corbin Neeley had gained consciousness and had left the O.R.

One of the paramedics came over to Gunter nodding his head in an affirmative gesture. "Are you the attending physician?"

"Yes," Gunter Hertzmann responded, "I am Dr. Gunter Hertzmann."

"You used sound judgment, doctor. Your patient is coming around but will need some additional time under your observation."

Within the next twenty minutes, all four paramedics had collected all their paraphernalia and disappeared.

Gunter assisted Verna into a bed in one of the hospital rooms. He noticed the awkward or painful appearing way she was struggling to walk. Gunter worried because he knew that any extended lithotomy positioning can be devastatingly dangerous. She was near exhaustion but was struggling to speak to Gunter.

"Thank you, Dr. Hertzmann. I just need to sleep for a little bit," she added as her eyes started closing.

"That is good, Verna. You just rest and if you need me or anything, ring the bell. You know that, of course."

Gunter still had a vicious feeling about Corbin and began a search of the entire facility. At this point, Gunter had no idea what he was going to do when he found Corbin. He had retained his mental stability but harbored an urge to hit or hurt Corbin in some way.

Before beginning his search. He left a note on Dr. Azran's desk that read URGENT, I MUST TALK TO YOU ASAP.

He searched every area of the clinic as well as sections of the hospital. In desperation, he went to the outside parking area and found Corbin's car was gone.

CHAPTER 26

REPLACEMENT SEARCH FOR CORBIN

D r. Azran returned to the clinic in the late afternoon and paged Gunter to meet him in his office. The ugly, sordid details of Corbin's activities and behavior were detailed by Gunter who was still livid when he told Dr. Azran that Corbin had doped Verna with an opioid cocktail.

"I'm thinking, Dr. Azran," Gunter said, "Corbin may never be seen here again in the clinic."

Dr. Azran interrupted, "He will never be allowed in this clinic ever. I want you to make a full report on every detail regarding this matter. Please have a copy on my desk by tomorrow morning and copy the police department."

"Dr. Azran, we will need to find another good physician possibly with with good surgical skills to replace Neeley."

"Yes, of course, Gunter, what are you thinking? Do you have someone in mind?"

"I do, sir. One of my classmates from Heidelberg has plans to leave Stuttgart and relocate here somewhere in California. In fact, he may have already relocated to California."

"Are you recommending this person?"

"Without hesitation, sir."

"What did you say his name was?

"Hartwig --- Helmut Hartwig, doctor."

"What are his strengths, Gunter?"

"Helmut Hartwig graduated med school in Germany with honors in internal medicine and is skilled in obstetrics and gynecology as well."

"Let's continue this further tomorrow. At this point, our focus must be resolving the damage and crime Corbin may have done."

"May I contact him and tell him that you might be interested in him?'

"Not immediately, Gunter. I want time to think over the situation with Corbin's flight."

Gunter work responsibilities had more than doubled since Corbin had exited. Corbin's electrical know-how gave him the ability to handle most any electrical problem that happened in the clinic or hospital. Thus, Gunter had gained a better understanding of Corbin's fascination of electro-magnetic devices and the potential applications as medical panaceas. Nevertheless, Gunter's more recent interactions with Corbin and the incident of Verna's introduction to opioids had planted a vitriolic seed in his mind. Every day since Corbin's disappearance, the newer daily work that in reality was done by Corbin fed the poisonous seed's growth.

The menial demands of dogs, cats, rabbits, and rodents in the Animal lab were disgruntling to Gunter and added cumulatively to his disgust of Corbin. Of the various aggravations of cleaning up over unappreciative, dumb animals, one animal had seemed to appreciate the food and treats provided from Gunter. The dog's name was Rommel and as a Doberman, he was a beautiful, shiny black color with a sense of loyalty that appealed to Gunter. Gunter spoke to Rommel in German assuming that anyone, human or dog, would understand the German language. When Gunter prepared any special treat for his new friend, he called him Erwin Rommel. The dog responded to either or both as long as his food was already in his food pan.

Gunter had finished feeding Rommel when he heard an alarm from the front office. He chose to disregard the alarm until he remembered that Verna was not at her duty station. Dr. Azran had made arrangements for Verna to go to a rehabilitation program. She resisted his kindness claiming that she was not using any drugs and her one-time, single expose to oxycontin was not her doing in the first place. Her resistance was for naught because when Dr. Azran had made any decision, he always stayed the course.

CHAPTER 27

BIOTHERM STRANGE MEMO TO STOCKHOLDERS

Within a week following the dinner meeting between Alex Bondurant and Max Becker, Alex constructed a plan to contact all Biotherm stockholders worldwide. His objective was intended to maintain effective communication between investors and all activities directly related to Biotherm with emphasis on financial ramifications

His strategy was to establish more effective relationships with investors by writing a document that would be relatively unrelated to annual reports. Biotherm's advertising agency made a strong and aggressive plea to the board of directors to allow such communication to be generated and controlled by them rather than solely by the company president. However, Alex was adamant about deliberate decision to exclude outside counsel including Hale Irving, from involvement. After deliberation, he advised Marcella to exclude parts I, II, and III --- copy Hale Irving on only part IV.

His letter to all stockholders follows:

> To: Biotherm Shareholders
> From: Alex Bondurant, Pres.\CEO
>
> This is not this year's annual report. This is a simple memorandum from me to each of you with a simple purpose, viz., to keep you current on a few major issues. This is not some kind of cash call or a stealthily planned means to convey bad news. To the contrary, it is my duty and pleasure to give you advance information on very positive activities within your company.

I. Clarence Harwood submitted his resignation from your board of directors due to a continuing health problem.

II. The Japanese subsidiary, Nihon Science, advises that they plan to submit a Tender Offer to buy a specified percentage of Biotherm shares and operate as an independent Japanese company. Biotherm, as a holding company, has no intention to allow the specified percentage to be obtained by Nihon Science. In fact, the performance of this Kyoto-based company is presently a financial deterrent to all stockholders. It is my intent to divest of this company. In event that you receive proxies or agree to sell your shares, I, personally, ask you to disregard such contacts from them or from any proxy intermediates.

III. Dinner with Max Becker, President\CEO of Gigatrax Ltd. last week. Biotherm and Gigatrax Ltd. are both healthy companies with outstanding growth potential. Gigatrax has developed large international markets in Europe, Asia, and the Latin American countries. Biotherm sales distribution within the United States, Canada, and Mexico has far outstripped similar efforts by Gigatrax Ltd. Some combined relationship between Biotherm and Gigatrax Ltd. would simultaneously solve aggravating problems and provide significant cost reductions as well as synergetic profitability. (Importantly, this is not public information and should not be read as any firm decisions.)

IV. The following information is shown as item IV because it lacks obvious return on investment as well as believability.

A hand-delivered communication was given to me as I parked my car in the Biotherm parking lot. The individual acting as messenger said and I quote, "This directive was put into my hand by Kim Jong Un who assigned me to take any measures necessary to hand this to you and only to you."

There was no further communication between the two of us. He did not introduce himself and after his only sentence, he was picked up by another car and they drove away.

I continued into my office placing the envelope on my desk without any intent to open it or to read some ruse, a poor joke or someone's idea of foolishness. I joined a business meeting that was already in process by 8:30. I mentioned the unusually shaped envelope that I had left on my desk to one of my vice-presidents. He felt it was one of the strangest or most hilarious things he had ever heard. However, he suggested that we go back to my office just for the laugh.

We read the letter cautiously word by word in detail. There on the signature line was the writer's name, Kim Jong Un and above the typed name was what appeared to be a handwritten signature. We decided that it was some kind of jest. Yet, there remained an uncertainty. I decided to call our legal counsel, Hale Irving. Expecting him to laugh at me and tell me to toss the letter into the waste can. To the contrary, he said, "Do not discuss any aspect of this with anyone and meet me at noon here in my office".

His legal opinion was to contact the U.S. Department of State. Our next instructions were to not discuss this matter or show the letter to anyone. We were advised that someone from the FBI would come by and take the letter for further investigation.

Hopefully, without letting any cats out of any bags, the essence of the communication from Kim Jong Un was his plan to present a Tender Offer to all Biotherm shareholders to offer four times market share for each share owned. The Tender asked for sixty percent minimum. Further, his scheme was to combine all Biotherm operations into a new facility and building in Pyongyang, DPRK.

In this communication, he had contacted Koryo Tours to handle all aspects of my visit to meet with him. A suite had been reserved at the Ryugyong Hotel which was known as the "105 Building" denoting 105 floors.

My apologies for any absurdities written in this memo.

Alex Bondurant, Pres./CEO

Carlton Herrick had discussed every aspect relating to this memo to stockholders. He had tried using his most polite chain of command personality trying to dissuade Alex from following through with such a wild idea. Alex would not pay any attention to Carlton's logic. In desperation, Carlton had finally said, "Alex, if this backfires or explodes, you can't say I failed to advise you."

Carlton met with Juliette in the coffee shop and explained the details of Alex's intentions.

Juliette stared at Carlton with a quizzical expression asking, "What is he thinking anyway?"

Carlton stared at the floor mumbling, "I just do not know, Julie. Maybe it is early Alzheimer's."

"Have you tried to change his mind in some way?"

"Yes, Julie, in every way and I'll keep at it until the mailing goes out. Hale Irving called me. He said he had a fax sent by Marcella. Hale asked me if I felt Alex was doing okay. He suggested that I spend some private time with Alex. He feels that Alex is just not sounding like Alex."

CHAPTER 28

EXECUTIVE BOARD OUSTS HARWOOD

It was mid-afternoon and a small group of "suits" including Ken Elwood, Mary Ethel Hayes, Jim Calder, James DeVue III and Hale Irving was milling around the bar which did not open until after 4 P.M.

Mary Ethel Hayes spoke up. "Does anyone know what we are doing here at The Sea? Mr. Irving, do you know what Alex has in mind for today?"

"No, Mrs. Hayes, we will have to await his arrival to learn that and this is not my show today."

"Well, I guess so. This restaurant is too expensive to eat here."

"Mary Ethel," teased Ken Elwood, "everyone knows that your husband left you more money than Carter's little Liver Pills."

"Well," Jim Calder sounded startled," look who just came in to pay the bar tab."

"Jim, you know that I know that the bar does not serve until after four." Alex welcomed each Board member individually before announcing, "The Executive Board meeting for today is relatively simple and straight forward. Each matter will be presented and every Board Member is expected to openly vote. Any particular matter may be designated as requiring closed, written responses. If no questions, we will retire to the assigned room."

As the group proceeded through a hallway leading to the various meeting rooms, Hale Irving stopped to question Alex. "I am not privileged to vote at any Board meeting. As usual, my responsibility is limited to keeping matters in compliance to the Articles of Incorporation as well as any related State of Federal laws."

Alex nodded his understanding and approval stating, "Yes, of course, Hale, but it is equally important that I am able to observe your reactions to any actions or comments by members of the Board."

"Alex, as a matter of habit, I routinely make notes. This allows me to review salient points at a later time. However, if you observe me placing my pen atop the desk --- that can be my indication that I have some concern overs the present matter or, for that matter, present decision."

The Executive Board meeting was scheduled for the Scalia Meeting Room in The Sea, an excellent, seafood restaurant in Palo Alto, California near Stanford University.

The Scalia Room had been thoroughly prepared for the Biotherm meeting. The unusual table had hidden microphones located around the table with each one actuated by a proximity switch. Coffee and tea services available and ready with a varied assortment of cakes, pastries, Danish, and bagels.

Alex Bondurant remained standing and announced the objectives for the Executive Board meeting today.

"Gentlemen --- and you too, Mary Ethel. Thank you for being available on such short notice. Planned topics are limited to two matters today. Neither matter is apt to be time-consuming.

'The first open matter requires a show of hands voting," Alex explained, "and your vote will be limited to either agree or oppose, but any show of two-handed indicates that more explanation is needed."

"Now, stockholder communication --- primarily informal, has shown interest in adding a new Board Member.

Carlton Herrick's name has been suggested."

Alex observed Hale Irving's pen dropped to the table top.

"The second matter is vital to any concern about changes in the Board. Therefore, we will defer any discussion about Carlton Herrick."

"Several stockholders have been vociferous about what they have described as Board inactivity. The more clamorous complainers happen to be significant equity holders."

Jim Calder was drumming his fingers on the table; Alex addressed him.

"Alright, Jim. I did not call for any vote, but go ahead speak up and get it off your mind."

"No, you did not call for a vote, Alex. You just did not define or clarify any matter whatsoever."

"Fine, Jim here is the the bottom line." Alex's hesitation and tone of voice revealed his irritation.

"Clarence Harwood is integral to the complaints. His positive contributions have dwindled steadily for the last two years."

Mary Ethel Hayes raised both hands waving her right hand like a school child wanting to answer the question.

"You have the floor, Mary Ethel." Alex sat down.

"Mr. Chairman, you don't need Board approval to fire Clarence. So, why are we here?"

Alex's demeanor changed to contemplation. "Yes, Mary Ethel, for that matter, I could have let Clarence go, but dismissal at hs level should not be due to any single opinion."

James De Vue III raised his hand and stood all in one movement.

"I make a motion to the Executive Board that Clarence Harwood is relieved of all present and future responsibilities related to Biotherm." De Vue III smiled and sat down,

"I second the motion." Jim Calder stated.

Mary Ethel raised her left hand with her index finger pointing upward. "Then, is a vote being called?"

Alex said, "Approve", all hands raised up.

Alex spoke again, "Disapprove? then he said, "clearly unanimous approval.

I congratulate this decision as one in the best interest of Biotherm and I move that I as Chairman and President carry out the decision as approved by the Board.

"I second the motion" spoken by Ken Elwood.

"Now, I ask that we move to discuss remaining issues". Alex commented.

Mary Ethel asked a question, "Can you tell us what issue in a few minutes, Alex?"

"Very briefly, Mary Ethel, yes," Alex said, "as of today, we need to replace the Board seat that was occupied by Clarence and as previously mentioned several blocks of stock --- I mean stockholders have suggested replacing Clarence with Carlton Herrick."

James DeVue III loudly interrupted the proceedings. "I make a move to postpone indefinitely any motion pending."

"I will second that motion on the floor" came from Ken Elwood.

Before a vote was called the postponement unanimously killed any further discussion.

Mary Ethel Hayes expressed her thinking. "I'm hungry and ready for my supper unless a motion is necessary."

"Same here, Mary Ethel." Ken Elwood agreed as he stood and started talking to Jim Calder.

Hale Irving shook hands with Alex explaining that he had a previous business dinner.

Casual chit chat and a few goodbyes were exchanged as a loud crash directed everyone's attention to the meeting room.

Clarence Harwood had crashed through the door screaming, "You lousy bunch of bastards," he shouted as he pointed a silver, 38 Smith and Wesson, Chief revolver, fanning it slowly at each person. Within milliseconds, Jim Calder grabbed Clarence and thrown a round-house punch from the floor hitting Clarence in the temple and dropping him to the floor.

Standing atop a table, Alex took command of the chaos and said, "I am asking that we all forget what just happened. Putting Clarence in jail or worse is not in our best interest. Jim, you just saved some lives here. I do not think Clarence had intent to actually shoot anyone. Jim, thanks for your fast action and now I'm asking for you and Ken Elwood to take charge and see if you can help Clarence. Again, can we all pretend this never happened?"

After a few short grumbles and complaints, a subtle agreement was made by each person.

"Good session, Alex." Ken Elwood said, "You got the job done today. I am a bit worried about you, Alex. We have been associated for a long time. You were in the hospital a short time ago. I know the angina pain that continues to be an aggravation to you. I know, too, that your cardiologist has recommended you begin taking it easier. Today, I noticed the stress that you were feeling. Frankly, Alex, I saw at one point, your hand was trembling, but I am not your doctor."

"Oh, come on, Ken. Didn't you know or feel the tense situation that just happened? Well, I did and maybe, my hands trembled a bit. No worry. Appreciate your concern anyway."

"Just concerned about you, Alex." Ken placed his arm around Alex's shoulders.

"And, by the way, my friend, you are not my doctor. Indeed, you are my friend. Angina is not Alzheimer's or a mental derangement, but when I fail to pay your invoices, then, you should start worrying."

CHAPTER 29

SEARCH FOR COVARI

Communication to the Azran Clinic for Febrile and Exotic disease had increased more recently. Contacts from Japan, China, Malaysia, Australia, Italy, Brazil, and Mexico were typically related to febrile disease, things with names like E. coli. The big influx of contacts primarily from California was unrelated to disease or disorders or, for that matter, anything associated with health.

Telephone calls were still received by Verna Kellar and her new assistant hired to help Verna during her rehabilitation from an alleged incident with oxycodone. Verna's helper kept a record of all telephone calls, emails, faxes, and written communication that inquired about Armand Covari.

The FDA from Silver Springs, Maryland alone had made six telephone calls to both Dr. Azran as well as Dr. Hertzmann. Police from numerous cities around the United States had made numerous inquiries. Four different FBI agents had personally visited and spoken to Dr. Azran and Gunter. Officer Warren who had previously been to Azran Clinic had returned twice. He had incisive questions about Corbin Neeley, but most questions related to Covari's whereabouts. Seven telephone calls from John Covari had been made to Dr. Azran, the last three were not transferred to Dr. Azran. After the seventh call, John Covari sent several wires to Dr. Azran. Mr. Covari had walked into the clinic unannounced asking to speak to Dr. Azran. Being advised that Dr. Azran was not available, he demanded that Dr. Hertzmann see him immediately.

Gunter had been instructed by the Clinic's legal counsel to say nothing whatsoever about Armand Covari and that if he was threatened in any way to refer the person to his legal counsel.

Verna had taken thirty to fifty calls per day herself. Her assistant was unable to respond to any matters that had happened previously. Verna had revealed all the intimate details of her experiences with Corbin Neeley to Gunter and he has assured her that he would take responsibility for the explant of the implanted, sound-wave oscillator.

John Covari entered the waiting room of the Azran Clinic just after the morning opening hours. Verna intercepted him before either Dr. Azran or Dr. Hertzmann had arrived. Mr. Covari introduced himself to Verna as John Covari Esq. and district attorney.

"Tell me, Miss ---," he stumbled.

"I'm Verna Kellar, Mr. Covari, and as I said to you before Dr. Azran has no knowledge of your son's whereabouts.'

"You said that. I know what you said, but I want to hear what you know --- not Azran."

"Mr. Covari, I do understand what a miserable feeling to not know where your son is or what happened to him, but if you think it has something to do with the Azran clinic, your assumption is way off base."

"Verna --- may I call you Verna?" He questioned.

Completely frustrated, Verna replied, "Sir, Dr. Hertzmann will talk with you if you like."

"Fine with me, Verna. Show me his office, please."

"He is with a patient, but when he is finished I will ask him to meet you here in the waiting room."

"Okay, Verna, my Son told me one of the docs here was in violation of FDA regulations. He said this doc was rude and attacked him viciously. What can you tell me about that, Verna?"

"Sir, I have no knowledge of any such event. Did he say which doctor? I doubt that it could have been anyone here.?"

Gunter walked into the room extending his hand, "I'm Gunter Hertzmann. I understand you are the father to the FDA inspector who calls on Azran Clinic."

"Yes, Doctor Hertzmann, I have initiated searches country-wide attempting to locate Armand. I hired a private investigator. Too, the FDA in Silver Springs informed me that Armand can not be located and they have advised the FBI to initiate an investigation."

"I can empathize with your frustration, Mr. Covari. The former M.D. was also a DVM ---"

"Did you say DVM? What is a DVM?" John Covari asked this with a quizzical expression.

"He is --- or was a doctor of veterinary medicine which may relate to your son's FDA responsibilities."?

"Dr. Hertzmann, empathizing can not resolve my concerns and fears. I have no information whatsoever about my son, his whereabouts, his health or wellbeing. In fact, no one is providing any information of value to me. It seems that my son never existed excepting vague rumors of his dislike and physical maltreatment of my son here in Azran Clinic."

"Mr. Covari, if I knew anything or could help you in any way, you would have my total support, but I was completely uninvolved in any aspect of FDA matters. You mentioned you have a private investigator?"

"Yes, thus far he has not uncovered any highly significant information about Armand. He had some rumors about a physical altercation with --- as he said one of the doctors here, but no details at all."

"Who was the other doctor here? John Covari continued his interrogation.

"Corbin Neeley, I knew him, yes, but not well. More importantly, he left here of hs own volition without any resignation, not even a goodbye. Dr. Azran was not even here when Dr. Neeley just packed up and left."

"If you learn where he is or how to get in touch with him, will you let me know?"

"I will should he contact me, but he has no motivation to communicate with me. I am sorry."

Another person entered the door as Verna walked away from her desk toward the new visitor.

"Good morning, sir. Welcome to Azran Clinic. Do you have a scheduled appointment this morning?"

"No, Verna, we talked several times on the phone. I'm Walter Dunn, an FBI agent as you may recall from our last telephone conversation." He emphasized his affiliation with the FBI.

"Excuse me, Mr. Dunn," John Covari interrupted, "let me introduce myself. I am John Covari, the County District Attorney."

"I do know who you are, Counselor. I got my J.D. --- ah, my law degree at the same place as you did, but years after you graduated".

Fortuitous to stumble onto you today. I had planned on calling your office to set up an appointment regarding your son, Armand.

"Gentlemen, I don't like being rude, but I have patients waiting in two exam rooms. You know how it feels when the doctor keeps you waiting." Gunter spoke but was already eight feet away.

"Thank you very much, Doctor Hertzmann. I appreciate your time." John Covari rotated back facing the FBI man.

"I need any information you might have about Armand, Mr. Dunn. I am aware that the Bureau has been investigating Armand's previous activities here at Azran Clinic. However, it seems that no one here knows anything or they are unwilling to divulge anything about Armand."

"Well, Mr. Covari, you and I both know that with legal ramifications possibly pending the Azran employees have been instructed to clam up."

"Mr. Dunn, as a fellow attorney, if you can give me a shred of data --- even let me know if Armand is alive and well, it would calm my wife, Armand's mother. His disappearance is totally unnerving to her." Covari pleaded.

CHAPTER 30

GYNECOLOGIST JOINS AZRAN CLINIC

The loss of Corbin Neeley created many changes in the operation of Azran Clinic. Foremost among changes was the unforeseen chaos, confusion and routine responsibilities that were no longer being handled automatically. The shortcomings Gunter spotted early on realizing that Corbin Neeley were doing a myriad of jobs that no longer were getting attention. Within the animal room, housekeeping had deteriorated to slovenly.

Dr. Azran had observed the condition and described it as messy, dirty and unacceptable. Bacterial infections were rampant amongst the rodent population. Dr. Azran had become dependent and reliable on everyone of his staff keeping control of any detail that might possibly detract his from his personal activities.

Gunter recognized that the time was right to remind Dr. Azran about the growing need to increase both the administrative staff in addition to another physician\surgeon.

Gunter called Dr. Azran on the intercom. "Dr. Azran, I'd like to discuss present operations with you. If you are available, I'd like to come into your office."

"Good idea, Gunter. You know that my door is always open. Come on in if you are ready."

"Thank you, Dr. Azran. I will be there momentarily, Dr. Azran."

"Gunter, isn't it about time you call me Harman?"

"Yes sir, Dr. Azran."

"Okay, Gunter, whenever you are ready."

Dr. Azran office was equipped with an automatic coffee-making system with choices of coffee, chocolate, cocoa, and assorted other drinks. As Gunter walked in he remained standing in front of Dr. Azran's desk.

"Grab a comfortable chair and fix yourself a coffee or whatever you prefer, Gunter."

Dr. Azran assisted Gunter in setting the coffee system for a Dark-Roasted Hawaiian Coffee. He then prepared a Camomile Tea for himself.

"I assume you want to talk about bringing on a replacement for Corbin, correct?"

"Yes sir, the demands are swamping me and without a good replacement, my own contributions become ineffective."

"How about your friend, Helmut Hartwig?'

"I will tell you about that. The only contact has been e-mail and Twitter and limited to friendly comments. You asked to defer any direct interaction for the time being."

"You know, Gunter, when you recommend a friend for a position, you become accountable for his performance. It takes more time and demands and creates more responsibilities for you."

"I can understand your warning," Gunter uttered, "he asked me about working here."

"Not a warning. I meant it as a caution," Azran stated, "are you willing to accept responsibility for bringing him on here reporting to you?"

"Totally, Dr. Azran."

"Call me Harman, okay? Then, call him and explain what we have just discussed. Then, arrange to get him here for his interview."

"What would be best day and time for you --- ah, Harman?"

"Any day next week around noon is best for me. My interview will be a cursory get acquainted only."

That early evening Gunter called Helmut Hartwig. After five rings, someone answered.

"Hello, this is Helmut Hartwig."

Gunter jumped right into the call, "Wie gehts, mein freund. Ich bin Gunter hier."

"English, please. I don't speak German anymore in the USA. So, ol' buddy, how are you."

"Good --- ah, very good, Helmut. Are you still interested in a job in the San Francisco Bay area?"

"Am I? Yes, indeed. I'm ready to get back to medicine. I'm not ready to flip burgers at McDonald's quite yet. I am ready to go anywhere for most any medical opportunity. What are you talking about?"

"Okay, Helmut, Dr. Azran promoted me and allows me to hire whomever I need. What do you think of that, Helmut?"

"I think that is great. Congratulations!"

"Well, you would be working for me --- that is, a part of my team. Are you still interested?"

"Well, of course, what do you need, Gunter?"

"Right off the bat, there is no obstetrics or gynecology at Azran Clinic. You would head up that department."

"Hey, Gunter, you say I would start off as a department head?"?

"Absolutely, of course, Helmut. There may be periodic gastroenterological surgeries like colonoscopies, but each such surgery earns a bonus."

"Sounds like my kinda' thing. Are we talking about a salary position?"

"Yes, but this has yet to be approved by Dr. Azran."

"Why don't you plan on coming on down, meet Azran and plan on looking for where you want to live. So, pack for the next few weeks. We will work out specifics when you are here."

"Great, Gunter. Appreciate this great opportunity. Working with you sounds wonderful. I will make travel arrangements and let you know my itinerary."

"Good, Helmut," Gunter said, "and do keep a record of your expenses. You are officially on expense now. Reimbursement will be fast."

"Gunter, I know I am going to have more questions and things to ask. Thank you again."

"Don't hang up yet, Helmut," Gunter demanded, "why don't you speak German anymore, Helmut?"

"Oh, it is no big thing. It is just that some time ago, I was performing a laparoscopic gall bladder surgery and the anesthesiologist, a fellow German spoke to me in our native language. Well, anyway, the rest of the surgical team revolted claiming that I had deliberately tried to keep them uninformed."

"Helmut, that makes no sense. I understand what you just explained. Still, most Americans do not speak any language other than English and, frankly, their English, generally, is not too good anyway. I'll say this, Helmut, here at Azran Clinic, you can speak German anytime the notion strikes you."

Helmut laughed saying, "Sehr gut, mein freund, vielen danke und auf weidersehen!"

"Helmut, I will explain in further detail but, I will ask you to do a freebie --- like the lawyers say, a pro bono for the clinic."

"No problem, is this some personal involvement, Gunter?"

"Oh, no, Helmut," Gunter responded, "It is an employee of Azran Clinic, Helmut."

"Fine, Gunter," Helmut said, "I do not need any details. If you ask, it will be done."

CHAPTER 31

AZRAN CLINIC MASSIVE POWER FAILURE

Verna's rapid recuperations had resulted in her ability to be the first arrival every working day at Azran Clinic. She had her own set of keys to the clinic and enjoyed opening up each morning. Her established habit after entering the front door was to turn on all the lights in sequence. After which, she checked the temperature and humidity in every part of the clinic. Verna had assumed responsibility for the Animal Lab since Corbin had disappeared and she now managed the watering and feeding schedules.

As she unlocked the front door, she observed the outside light above the front door was not working. It was a night light and set to shut off at first daylight. She decided to check the switch when she was inside. She entered and closed the door after herself and reached to try the switch for the outside light. She changed the switch off and on repeatedly without any result. In frustration, Verna pushed the array of all switches adjacent to the outside light switch. The room remained dark with the only sunlight just coming through the windows.

Verna's sense of responsibility and dedication were subdued by a flash of panic. She was afraid that patients in the hospital section may be in trouble until she remembered that he hospital had a self-powered, automatic electrical system. Hospital lights would all be okay.

"Damn it," she said aloud, "why didn't they hook up the clinic like that."

Her next thought was 'fuses and circuit-breakers'. The following thought was the realization that she knew absolutely nothing about either fuses or circuit breakers.

She rushed back outside searching for Jesse. Verna saw him just getting out of his car and pinching a bit of dip to place into his cheek before closing his car door. She rushed toward him shouting, "Hey, Jesse, I need help inside, Jesse!" She motioned to have Jesse follow her.

Again, inside the waiting room, Jesse asked, "What is the matter?"

Verna appeared to be flustered. "I don't know, Jesse," she blurted, "all the lights are out."

"I maybe can fix that. Do you know where the fuse box is?"

"I have no idea, Jesse."

"That is okay, I'll look for it." Jessie smiled.

Jesse spent the next half-hour searching inside the clinic opening doors and looking outside the building.

When Verna found him walking around the outside of the building, she asked, "Did you find it, Jesse?"

"Nope, no ma'am, I sure looked but I couldn't find it, but I have a good idea."

"Okay, Jesse, I am all ears. Are you going to let me know your idea?"

"Well, the hospital section has a resident engineer that knows his business. You can call him if you want."

"You probably should talk to him since you already know him, Jesse, okay?" Verna tried pleading.

"If you ask him, he will do it right away. If I ask him, he will probably tell me to do it myself or wait until he has nothing else to do."

Verna went again to the electric switches in the waiting room before calling the hospital engineer. When she called, she learned that the engineer was on coffee break and might call her after his coffee break.

"Emergency", Verna emphasized, "this is a serious matter. I need help now or I'll have to call the Fire Department."

"Don't do that," the voice suggested, "I can go get him immediately and he can be there in minutes."

The engineer arrived with an assortment of tools and meters asking, "What is your problem?"

"It is not my problem, but if we don't get the power back on it will be Dr. Azran's problem. Too, mister what ever your name is, I don't know where the fuses are located."

"I do," he said, but fuses are from yesterday. I know where the circuit breaker panel is located and I'm on my way. I'll call just as soon as I reset the circuit breakers that must have gotten overloaded."

After about an hour later, Dr. Azran and Gunter arrived to find all power was off throughout the clinic. Verna explained that she was on top of the problem and the hospital engineer was fixing it at this precise minute.

Dr. Azran spoke to Gunter, "Probably just some minor nuisance. Let's go out for coffee and you can tell me about the conversation with your friend, Dr. Hartwig."

Verna held up an index finger, "Do you want me to stay in the office?"

"No, Verna, not necessary. I will contact the hospital engineer and find out what the problem was. Anyway, take off the day and we will let you know when the power is back on." Dr. Azran usually gave clear instructions.

Dr. Azran and Dr. Hertzmann opted for some breakfast rather than for just coffee. They and had a long conversation about hiring Helmut Hartwig. The addition of a talented. experienced gynecologist and obstetrician had unquestioned values. The increased medical capabilities would open up an attractive female market segment.

Dr. Azran's cell phone signaled for his attention, but he had chosen to defer all messages during his conversation with Gunter. After the fifth or sixth signal, Dr. Azran excused himself to take the insistent caller.

"Pardon me, Gunter, this may be the hospital engineer. I had left my number on his answering service before we left earlier."

"Hello, this is Dr. Azran."

"Oh, good, Dr. Azran --- this is the Hospital Engineer and the news may not be so good. The damage is best described as extensive. Yes, the circuit breaker had tripped, but the consequences of that is another matter."

"Please, continue, have you been successful in restoring power to the clinic?"

"No, doctor, the damage is well above my ability to reinstate power. The causative agent could have been some device or instrument or system that demanded exceedingly high wattage. I measured amperage that I suspected as being related to the failure. Ten amps is big, no question. However, the total power, that is, wattage, virtually melted some copper wiring ---"

"You are telling me more than I need to know with your engineering language. My question is simple. Can you repair the damage and have the clinic up and running as soon as possible?"

"No, sir, not a remote possibility. In my professional opinion, the optimum solution is to assign this to either a general contractor or maybe, an electrical contractor with high voltage, high power experience."

"It does not sound like the best news. Can you recommend a good electrical contractor?"

"I might give you an opinion, doctor, but this kind of failure is beyond my education and experience. I will call you with my ideas later today. Sorry, I could not help more."

Gunter and Harman sat staring at their now cold drinks and commiserating about their mutual problems.

"I can get you another hot tea, Harman, if you want some more, Gunter offered,"

"I really do not want any more, Gunter," Harman mumbled, "and Gunter, another thing, Your friend, Helmut, will arrive in a few days. His impressions are not apt to be favorable with the present mess in the clinic."

"I'd not be concerned about Helmut. He is so excited about working with us, a little mess just will not bother him."

CHAPTER 32

ALEX, MAX, AND CARLTON AT ESCONDIDO

The atmosphere at Maurice's had the feel of a small, European restaurant that offered privacy, comfort and the ultimate in French delicacies. Maurice owned several unique restaurants. One called Gastronomique was a very exclusive and very expensive restaurant exclusively for members and guests of members. Uniquely, no advertising or promotions were even considered for this restaurant. The location was as uniquely centered in the center a large farm area attempting to grow avocados which seemed unusual since Spanish or Latin American foods were rarely if ever, served. Intentionally hidden from the public or casual drivers by consecutive right and left turns like a maze. Both Alex and Max were members of both of Maurice'sestablishents. They both had expressed their choice for Escondido. The name of the establishment, Escondido, was known only to a chosen profile of well-heeled patrons who paid initial membership fees of one thousand dollars. To any common person, it was unknown and unaffordable.

Max arrived a few minutes early and was escorted to the bar by Maurice who introduced him to the bartender with an understood, "Mr. Becker is my very good friend". Maurice headed back to the bolted front door to await arrival by Alex. Max was studying the lemon peel on his gin martini wondering if Alex and Carlton were in agreement.

Maurice was rarely to be seen at Escondido. It was not a French restaurant and decidedly never offered Latino specialties. Conversely, Maurice spent much of his time at Gastronomique as executive chef, sous chef or if he preferred, sommelier if a rare French wine was ordered. He spent time often near the cocktail bar explaining the bullet holes in the mirror behind the various liquors. On occasion, he manned the locked, front door that required knocking with a cast iron door knocker to gain entrance but, only when he was expecting royalty, friends or big name celebrities.

Both Alex Bondurant and Max Becker have comped lifetime membership to Gastronomique; neither was an over-indulgent gourmand and they were always warmly welcomed by Maurice and surprised when he prepared a special recipe and delivered it to their table.

Tonight, Max had contacted Maurice to establish the dinner menu, especially for etouffee.

It was a masterpiece in Maurice's hands. Nevertheless, Maurice had developed an appreciated courtesy of reminding important customers of his ingredients and special handling requirements of dishes as unique as E'Touffee.

Too, Maurice had been a Sommelier well before he developed into a world famous Executive Chef and he routinely selected the wine to be served with any of his own renowned specialties. Tonight, Maurice had flown in a Louis Latour Puligny-Montrachet, vintage 2012 from the Burgundy region of France. It was unimaginable that any wine connoisseur might make an improper comment about Maurice's selection.

Alex arrived with Carlton who gushed with apologies about being a few minutes late because of traffic, real or imagined.

Alex and Max knew each other's habits and what each preferred to drink. Max had already ordered gin martinis both with lemon twists. As the drinks were placed on their table, Max held up his index finger to focus attention on himself.

"Alex, let us clink our glasses as we bring up a discomforting matter that has been brought to my attention. Is it a fact that you forced Clarence Harwood off of your board and withdrew his unvested options?"

"Yes, Max. It is a long overdue action that I had postponed too long. Is this going to cause you anguish or detract from our E'Touffee?"

"Alex, I have never questioned decisions that you made and do not intend to do so now."

"Max, I am surprised that you already know of an event that will not happen until next week."

"I suggest we not dwell on who said what to whom, Alex. Our talk tonight is of far greater significance."

"Thank you, Max. It is vital that we maintain our long friendship. Add him to your board over at Gigatrax if you feel you need him."

"He was on your board for a long time, Alex. Why are you dismissing him after all this time?"

"As my excuse, call it a management weakness or a simple faux pas, Max. Simply put, his contributions have been deteriorating for the last two years. It is not a decision that I feel proud about but it was requisite."

"Add Clarence to my Board? Nope, thank you, Alex, if you chose to dismiss Clarence, why would I even consider adding excess baggage to my board?"

"Okay, we will be enjoying our French\Cajun dinner in minutes. Is it Cajun?"

"Not sure. It is one of the greatest tasting dishes ever --- whatever its ethnic heritage." Alex added.

"Well, gentlemen, this may be a good time to order another drink," Max said," some of the points or suggestions, if you will, might be very distressing or annoying to either of you --- or, for that matter, to both of you. However, I want to begin our discussion with a pact that we three will not share any aspect of tonight's conversation with anyone. And, my fellow compatriots, any ideas or concepts that we talk about must not be shared with any wife or family member. Am I completely clear? If such a blood pact is acceptable to you, a handshake will open our discussion."

A three-way handshake accompanied the favorable nods of all three heads.

Carlton interrupted, "Good prelude, Max, you have my rapt focus and attention."

"Absolutely," Alex agreed, "I am anxious to hear everything you are about to say."

"Okay, good, Alex --- you too, Carlton. You are vital and integral parts of this whole plan. Now, the intended bottom line will be financially favorable to our respective companies as well make each of us and our families totally solvent. I mean to say that as dedicated, senior executives, we, each, have earned far more ROI than actually received."

"Excuse me, Max," Carlton injected, "I'd like you to begin for my benefit, what is the objective?"

"Fine question, Carlton. Alex warned me that you were an astute analyzer and would have questions no matter the topic. So, Alex also mentioned he was considering a vice-presidency for you at the next board meeting. Simply put, Carlton, I believe I have a much better idea and a unique title for you with substantially more money and perqs."

"As I said earlier, Max, you have my full attention."

"First, Carlton, vital that you know that Alex is planning to retire and he tells me sooner than later."

"Surprise? I can understand that but still, I feel a mite flabbergasted."

Max pointed to Carlton. "This is where your star rises, Carlton. I feel we should combine our operations by Gigatrax making a very attractive Tender Offer to acquire controlling interest in Biotherm as a subsidiary of Gigatrax and you as Sr. Executive Officer. The new title comes with a cash bonus of two hundred thousand dollars, new company car of your choice, an off-site apartment in San Francisco for entertainment, innumerable perqs plus a series of stock options over your tenure with annual vesting of ten to twenty percent as you determine appropriate. I am nominated as Chairman of the resultant company which obviously opens, even more, growth potential for you."

"Way beyond anything I might have ever imagined. Do I like the sounds of what I am hearing? Well, hell, yes! Yet, is this thinking collusion or a deliberate Insider Trading scheme?" Carlton brow became a deep furrow.

"Your valid concerns will be legally accomplished to your satisfaction using off-shore entities that are already in position."

"Too, what will be our relationship and interactions with Alex?" Carlton's expression showed deep concern.

"Alex has agreed to accept five million dollars to assist in completing these plans and to remain available for consultation --- at a continuing fee, of course. Alex is talking about living in the Keys."

"Max, your explanation has been stellar. I do, as you observe, have several concerns which I prefer to discuss with Alex. That would not violate our solvency pact --- true?"

"Yes, do you want to discuss with Alex right now?"

"At this precise second? No. Too, my Pres.\CEO salary has not been mentioned, Max."

"Does $1,500,000 per year payable float your boat? Paid to an offshore account sound good sound to you?"

"I had heard, Max, that you knew how to close sales. But, still, want to sit and talk to Alex later."

Not a single one of the trio had any recollection of having E'Toufee for dinner.

"One other matter," Max explained," I have biographical summaries on Board Members from my --- that is, Gigatrax as well as Biotherm. I'm suggesting that a new Board of Directors must be created. Gigatrax has three members at present. Biotherm, if I am correct, has four now. Is that right, Alex?"

"It was five until Clarence was voted off, Max," Alex confirmed, "Yes, it is four."

"Therefore, we have seven candidates theoretically. Our new, combined company can easily justify a ten person board. Concurrently, not all current directors have been stellar performers.?

Carlton spoke up, "The timing is optimum to separate the wheat from the chaff. Is this your thinking, Max?"

"Absolutely, Carlton. In the interest of time, I will read the name of each board member and a show of up ur down members will provide some guidance regarding our new board. Then, if any two thumbs up will be nominated. Conversely, any two thumbs down requires an exit strategy. Agree?"

Max started reading. "Number 1--- Jim Calder?" The result was three favorable.

Max continued, "Number 2 --- James DeVue?" The result was two favorable.

"Number 3 --- Ken Elwood?" The result was not determined.

"Number 4 --- Mary Ethel Hayes?" The result was two down thumbs.

"Number 5 --- K. B. Randall?" The result was two thumbs up.

"Number 6 --- Kenny McMasters?" The result was two thumbs up.

Max read the last candidate. "Number 7 --- Fred Terman?" The result was two thumbs down.

"I suggest, "Max requested "that the method used for nomination and the actual vote remain confidential. In conclusion for the day, let me know your opinion of Kenny McMasters.

CHAPTER 33

NEW BOARD MEETS IN SAN FRANCISCO

Resulting from the dinner meeting between Max Becker, Alex Bondurant, and Carlton Herrick, a detailed plan of action was being developed in infinite detail.

After an inordinate amount of discussion between these three executives an assortment of decisions were presented and as each idea was described, it would be relegated to the left side as assets or to the right side as liabilities. They had agreed on a rule of thumb that all decisions should be measured toward the objective of enhancing the company equity. The so-called "Ben Franklin Balance Sheet" proved to be the most effective way to minimize personal choices or strong biases. Too, the three-way effort fortified the worthiness of any given aspect of the plan.

Max Becker placed his pen on the table. Alex and Carlton recognized his habit of laying down his pen before beginning an important statement. They both seemed to relax as each adjusted to more comfortable positions in their chairs.

"We all recognize that a new board of directors is badly needed and simultaneously we have a few seasoned directors that are still capable of worthy contributions. I suggest we separate the wheat from the chaff early on by buying back equity ---.

Carlton spoke a bit early, "Max, I could place that suggestion on the left side of the balance sheet on the basis that if we can counter the buyback expense liability with a fresh infusion of investment capital."

"Can't disagree," Max says, "after the buyback, we divest of equity that we are holding by offering new investments in the newly structured company, that is a choice between common or preferred stock."

Alex entered the conversation. "I think Max's idea has merit. For one, it is good sales skill to always offer the prospect a choice between something or something else rather than a choice between something or nothing."

"So, Alex", Carlton spoke, "a preferred choice is a sound concept, correct?"

"No," Carlton," Alex corrected, "not necessarily."

"Alex, remember that finance and economics are not my things. Explain your last remark, please."

"Preferred stock to me means to me that the owner gets no voting privileges. Preferred is a position between investment in bonds and common stock. Me? I like the chances of growing with the company which in my opinion is not good as owning common."

"Well, Alex, let me give you an amen. Any optional choice between fits your idea of good salesmanship."

"Yes, indeed, Max." A good sales manager from years ago taught me that. Too, I recall that he made decisions like a machine gun."

Carlton added, "Sounds good to me, but machine gun decisions are only bad when they are wrong."

Max chuckled. "Un huh, been there, done that. Let's move ahead."

"My time is measurable with the company. I'd like very much to meet with the new Board and be permitted to welcome them and to advise them that their board chairs are symbols of success and power yet temporary until sanctioned by stockholders next annual meeting" Alex asked for this consideration.

"To be expected, Alex, you earned that right. Where would you like to hold this meeting?" Max asked.

"I had not given any thought to that question. Carlton, any recommendations?"

"Sure, as long as it is not in Ojai, California. Conversely, French Quarter in New Orleans is not even close to a business orientation. Still, it should be memorable in my opinion."

"What about a financially oriented setting in a major city like San Francisco?" Max expressed his choice.

Carlton seconded the motion, "Definitely left side balance sheet, Max."

"From your description of a good place, I am unable to even suggest a more appropriate spot other the Palace Hotel on New Montgomery in San Francisco. If memory serves me, I think it is located in the financial district. It offers luxurious rooms and services are the best. If it fits our Ben Franklin Balance sheet, a dinner look-see would be well-rewarded."

Alex began by nodding his head in approval. "I know the Palace Hotel. As perfect as it can get in my opinion if it fits our budget."

Days became weeks and the entire project was assigned to three senior employees of Gigatrax who negotiated the activity to a professional planning organization.

Five prospects for the newly organized board arrived the early evening before the date of the meeting.

Kenny McMasters and K. B. Randall had arrived together, been assigned to a premier services floor, unpacked, freshened up, and agreed to meet in the cocktail lounge around 5 o'clock. The ex-Biotherm board members Jim Calder, James DeVue, and Kenneth Elwood had gathered near an old haunt that had been known as Rickey's Hyatt House on El Camino Real. When Rickey's closed in 2005, Dinah's Garden Hotel became even more popular. The ex-Biotherm board would convene here and arrange transportation.

Jim Calder convinced Elwood and DeVue that arriving at the Palace Hotel in an expensive limousine might be viewed as impetuous and extravagant. He volunteered to act as chauffeur. They readily accepted.

By six-fifteen that night, all five had gathered in the cocktail lounge reintroducing each other and asking questions or making references to the meeting tomorrow.

All five attendees stood in a circle exchanging opinions, viewpoints, and comments.

Kenny McMasters spoke, "I notice as I look around at the faces in our circle that a few people I expected to see are missing."

"I'm glad you mentioned that Kenny," Jim Calder said," I wonder how such decisions were made."

"Executive decision must be the answer to the question, Jim." Kenneth Elwood answered.

"Well, anyway, I do not know how others felt about Clarence Harwood, but I always believed he was a laggard. Meaningful contributions from him were few and far between." Jim Calder volunteered.

"You know, Jim, that opinion you just stated answered your comments about how decisions get made," McMasters chided, "rock throwing at the decisions of others is not a good habit."

"I know, Kenny I agree and apologize." Calder thanks, McMasters.

"Okay, I have to say that I will miss Mary Ethel. She had plenty of dedication." James DeVue commented.

"Yes, she did. However, she wasn't on the chopping block. To the contrary, she planned to resign from the board and Alex simply followed her wishes." Calder settled any further questions.

Kenny McMasters steered the comments another direction. "Gentlemen --- oops, sorry K.B. I didn't forget about you. We all must consider that we have no free passes or guarantees of a lifetime membership to the new board. First, we have yet to be appointed. So, until the next annual stockholders' meeting, we may be occupying chairs that belong to someone else."

K. B. Randall had been silently observant. She addressed McMasters. "Kenny, unless your cruise ship sinks, you have few concerns and zero worries from my vantage point. Genomix stock is bluer than blue with the Dow Jones, S and P, and Nasdaq all showing near unbelievable highs."

"I will respond to your compliment if that was your intent, after the meeting tomorrow."

"Touche, Kenny!"

Morning came early with a thin layer of fog which would dominate most breakfasts conversations in San Francisco.

McMasters and Randall sat together with both opting for the sumptuous buffet. Breakfast table service was impeccable. Two waiters were assigned to their table. The waiters already knew the names of both people they were serving. Randall's tea service was constantly refreshed as was McMasters' coffee.

"The rooms on the special services floor are wonderful, aren't they, Kenny?"

"Yes, I'll say. The six shower heads with separate temperature control were impressive."

"Do you expect that every room has six shower heads?"

"I'd doubt that but maybe on the special services floor. Who knows?"

"Kenny, did you notice the Biotherm guys are sitting alone at their own table?"

"Probably have some private things or concerns to talk about, I'd guess."

"Do you think we should walk over and join them?"

Kenny frowned with his eyes and said, "Go ahead if you choose. I am going up to my room to take care of some Genomix business."

"See you at the meeting at 9:30." K. B. said as she stood and walked toward the other table.

All three, Ken Elwood, James DeVue, and Kenneth Elwood rose from their seats and acknowledge K. B. approaching.

Elwood invited K. B., "Join us, K. B., please. Our waiter is preparing what he described as The Palace Seasoned Demitasse for us."

"Oh, oh, sounds like something boozy. I think I'll pass and stay alert for our meeting today." K. B. announced.

"We asked. The waiter said no alcohol just organic spices."

Breakfast discussion continued with only casual references to the meeting today. After too many demitasses, the conversation went into a hyper-drive with casual talk about Clarence Harwood and relationships with Max Becker.

All participants were awaiting the meeting room door to be opened.

At precisely 9:30, the doors were opened.

Max was standing at the podium surveying the participants as they scanned the room for a seat.

"You all know me or know of me. Your opinion of me is of little concern to me. As your President and Chief Executive, the performance of our company should be the determining factor of your opinion of me. As a previous Board member, nothing has changed. You were never an employee per se. However, you were either contributing to your company or had the potential to make a significant contribution. In the following weeks, decisions will affect your compensation, perquisites and, possibly, your equity in the newly structured corporation --- do you have a question, Kenny?"

"What will board members equity be based upon?" McMasters questioned.

"Kenny, I intend to reserve answers to all questions for a specific Q and A sessions. Thus, I am deferring your answer until then, but I will make a few related comments which I will enumerate now.

1. Board Member compensation of companies with current ratios comparable to ours will be analyzed. The derived arithmetic mean will be a common amount to each member of the board. Comparisons and kibitzing over differences between individual board members will not be tolerated.
2. Allocations to board members will require purpose and standard expense reporting. Travel and anticipated expenses must be approved prior to any allocation. For example, air travel is limited to standard fares.
3. Your board chair is a privilege without a contractual agreement.
4. The newly formed organization is financially strong and growing, the board will be expanded to, at least, seven, possibly, nine members.
5. Membership to the board is subject to stockholder approval. Opinions, alliances or outside recommendations will not be considered. Such voting for Board Members will happen yearly at the stockholders meeting.

Max stepped back from the podium and the microphone as he spoke, "This group is small. Can everyone hear me perfectly? Good, we can talk better at the conference table. However, before changing chairs or positions, I want Alex Bondurant to take the floor. He can tell you about matters about some things that I cannot."

A round of applause greeted Alex as he stood. Max handed him the microphone.

"I won't need the mic, Max. My comments will be brief and as you asked, I, too, will ask that any questions be deferred until our Q and A session. Now, rumors about mergers, take-overs and about me have been circulating at an increased frequency of late. The age of 80 is still ahead of me. My cardiologist tells me that I am reasonably strong and healthy. With his next breath, he belabors about my chest pains as he calls angina. Then, he gets empathetic and whispers softly that if I hope to reach 80 years of age, I need to retire. He emphasized now."

"Max, I'd like to suggest a twenty-minute break before our Q and A session."

The group gave Alex a rousing round of applause and plenty of pats on his back.

CHAPTER 34

DISGRUNTLED BOARD MEMBERS

Fred Terman was ignominiously extracted from the Gigatrax Board of Directors. He had not graciously accepted the terms and conditions of his departure and had initiated a strategic campaign to regain whatever support possible by a deluge of emails, letters, and late night telephone calls to all the members of Gigatrax and Biotherm. Fred Terman's primary strategy was to attack the easiest targets to cause as much disgruntlement as possible while concurrently suggesting attractive financial plums for Board members who might be easily swayed.

Terman was envious and resentful when he first heard the rumors of a vice-presidency for Carlton Herrick. He suspected that K. B. Randall would be an easy target as well. He had joked about her attractions as being the most significant factors in her vice-presidency as chief financial officer and other lascivious remarks about her sexual attractions.

Terman had belittled Max Becker for sending his sensuous pet to New Orleans to get competitive market information from Biotherm. His philosophy was that beauty was not a requirement for any management position. Clearly, Terman was a practicing misogynist hoping to arouse like feeling among other male Board members.

It could not have been clear to see what end result Terman might have expected. In letters, to each and every former Board member, he had made lewd and highly suggested acquisitions of K. B. Randall's sexual activities as well as her shortcomings and failures as a Certified Tax Account.

In succession, of emails, Terman had belittled and besmirched Carlton Herrick's unjustifiable, rapid rise to the corporate level.

After multiple attacks on both K. B. Randall and Carlton Herrick, Terman arranged a conference call that included Kenny McMasters, James Calder, Ken Elwood, and James De Vue.

At 7:30 PM, the conference call was fully connected.

"This is Fred Terman. As I pronounce your name, please just repeat your name to be sure everyone is hearing you."

"Jim Calder ---"

"Yes, this is Jim."

"James DeVue ---"

"James De Vue --- hear you fine."

"Ken Elwood ---"

"Ken Elwood, okay for me."

"K. B. Randall ---"

"This is K. B. and I only have a minute or so."

"Kenny McMasters ---"

"Kenny McMasters --- let's get on with it, Fred"

"Fine, everybody, I'm sure that you --- every one of you must be concerned with the machinations of the recent reorganization. I think you will agree that the newly structured organization changes management and direction more than most folks change socks. I want to remind you that not every Board member has the same contract with the company. As a matter of fact, currently, I'm guessing that not one of you has a new Gigatrax contract for Board membership ---"

K. B. Randall interrupted, "Fred, is this conference call have some objective?"

"Just listen. My purpose will be as clear as rain water." Terman added.

"Okay, you all responded to the conference call," Terman said, "I know you have more questions than answers."

Jim Calder interrupted, "I have no time for pathetic complaints or sour grapes stories." His line clicked off.

"Same old Jim Calder. So, here is what you need to consider. Carlton Herrick, the executive without a title, is in Kyoto Japan in the midst of commandeering Nihon Science. He is in the midst of making organizational changes without any Board direction or sanction."

"Listen, Fred, the Board is not a part of line management. We are administrative advisory," K. B. stated emphatically, "Goodbye". Another line clicked off the conference call.

"So be it. She is no more than Max Becker's tart or Herrick's plaything anyway. So listen carefully before Herrick dissolves the entire Board of Directors." Terman demanded.

Terman waited for any response. He listened for questions or objection. The only sound was the dial tone.

CHAPTER 35

POWER FAILURE OPENS PANDORA'S BOX

The hospital engineer had done some private investigations and made several recommendations. Dr. Azner had assigned the task of locating an electrical contractor to Gunter and contracting with them to get the clinic back on line within the shortest amount of time.

Gunter had discussed the gravity of the situation with Verna and assigned her the responsibility to locate facilities capable of housing, feeding, watering, medicating and providing care and safety to the wide variety of animals in the animal lab.

Gunter investigations identified three reputable electrical contracts that agreed to come to the clinic and make estimates of costs to remedy the failures and restore the facilities to full capability. Gunter had demanded restoration with details of each phase of labor.

One company called Vast Engineering Solutions impressed Gunter with a significant factor. They convinced Gunter that hiring any single engineer with any single engineering background would be an expensive mistake. This company boasted that from the beginning, they would assign four professional engineers on the assignment. Specifically, they agreed that two electrical engineers, one mechanical engineer, and one industrial engineer would comprise the remediation team. Further, they agree that any unforeseen repairs would be included within the initial cost estimate.

One aspect of the initial agreement related to complex, expensive instrumentation that Vast Engineering would not accept liability viz., any medical devices and\or instruments under warranty would be excluded from the contract.

Gunter met with this team and negotiated a min-max estimate that impressed Dr. Azran.

The contract with Vast Engineering was approved by both Gunter and the funding allocated by Dr. Azran.

An initial team of four Vast Engineering specialists arrived immediately after the contract was in place and began their examination of all aspects of the power failure.

For the next six days, at least, one of the engineers worked around the clock. During daylight hours, all four engineers inspected, analyzed and discussed their findings. At four-thirty on every work day, a master document was updated that listed any and all problems or simple malfunctions. The objective that the team had defined was that the master document when meticulously arrayed with most significant problems first and incidentals at the bottom. The master report was routinely discussed with Gunter.

All electrical devices were inspected and adjusted to meet the manufacturer's specifications. Before each modification or change, the associated engineer has Gunter sign-off on all details.

Medical devices and instruments under warranty were isolated and tagged as NOT TESTED.

"This is the engineer from Vast Engineering Systems calling back, Doctor Azran. I talked to my supervisor and explained that I had just spoken to you a few minutes ago."

"He asked if I had brought you up to date on the clinic and when I told him that I decided to defer any info until tomorrow or later, He snapped back at me reminding me that withholding vital data is unacceptable. So, he said, 'Call him back right now and keep him totally informed. Am I clear?'

"No explanation is necessary. What was the info that you failed to give me?" Dr. Azran replied.

"Yes, sir, I apologize. All the Vast Engineering Systems team plus two of our senior physicists met and developed a list of problems that may still be the central cause of the total shut down."

"And ---, Dr. Azran was losing patience, "please, get to the point."

"Yes, doctor, we know the etiology of the entire electrical and thermal damages."

"And ---," Azran grumbled, "is the team initiating the fix or remedy to our problems?"

"Well, no, sir." The answer was almost whispered.

"Well, damn. Why Not?"

"Answer is relatively simple, doc. We located the greatest energy eater in all of the clinic, but the device is under warranty and when we called the manufacturer, they emphatically said that if we touched anything whatsoever, the warranty would be void."

"Who said that and what device caused this debacle?"

"It was and remains to be the L & N Crematory furnace. They told us they would get in touch with you and their service engineers would be there in a day or two."

"Azran was visibly irritated. Standing up he asked, "Is that all they said?"

"Well, he said for us to keep our hands off the system and advise our other engineers to do the same."

"I want the work being done by Vast Engineering to be halted until we discuss our warranty on the Crematory furnace. Dr. Hertzmann will keep you informed on the L & N cooperation."

"Gunter, I'd like you to make a conference call to L & N, Vast Engineering, and our Hospital Engineer including me and --- of course, yourself."

"Yes, sir. I will initiate the conference call and use our cell phones, okay?"

"Okay, clinic phones may not be available as much as I would rather be at my own desk." Harman complained.

Gunter setup the conference call and all recipients were on the line as Gunter set the stage.

"This is Dr. Gunter Hertzmann speaking from Azran Clinic. Vast Engineering has been retained to resolve a massive power failure here in the clinic. They have identified and isolated the source of the entire problem to our BLI-400 cremation device which is under warranty. Contact information between L & N and Vast Engineering should be exchanged. Dr. Azran asks that this matter gets resolved as quickly as possible with full power and with one-hundred percent operational capability."

"Doctor, this is, Joe Farrow at L & N. I'm Director of Field Engineering. Be assured that L & N will respond to your dilemma within the next sixty minutes. Advise personnel that our Field Engineers will arrive at Azran before three o'clock this afternoon. They should be authorized to work around the clock and have you operational quickly."

Gunter interrupted. "You all have my cell phone number. Contact me if you need more information. Thank you and I will say goodbye and get back to my patients now."

Minutes after 2:30, a panel truck marked L & N SYSTEMS pulled in the Azran parking lot, unpacked numerous equipment onto a mobile table while one of the occupants walked to the front entrance of Azran Clinic. He wore a uniform with L & N embroidered colorfully on his shirt. Over the left front pocket, the same embroidery spelled the name JEFF.

Verna was sitting on a bench at the front door and approached Jeff saying, "Dr. Azran is not available today".

Jeff tipped his ball cap and spoke, "We already talked to Dr. Azran and to Dr. Hertzmann about beginning work on your BLI- 400."

"That's okay, but we have no power or lights", she said.

"No problem, miss, we have our own generator and all the equipment being loaded off our truck. I'm Jeff and we may be working some long hours --- even all night."

The following morning, Dr. Azran and Dr. Hertzmann arrived together. It was close to 10 AM and three Field Engineers including Jeff were still outside sitting on the bench.

"Good morning, gentlemen," Dr. Azran spoke acknowledging each of the men, "You got here early this morning."

"No, sir," all three spoke in unplanned harmony," we worked all night."

The largest man of the three addressed Dr. Azran, "And, doctor, frankly, I am exhausted."

"I can see that all three of you are tired and I do appreciate your obvious dedication."

"We have complete details that you need to understand, doctor. We can continue the discussion at our office or, if you prefer, give you a flash report right here."

"Right here is good for us. I can have Verna order out for some coffee or something to eat."

"Frankly, doctor, here is better for us because we can get home for a few hours of sleep."

Jeff started, "Doctor, the results are not pleasurable to even discuss. However, I will enumerate point by point. I do have a question for you."

"Go ahead, you have aroused my attention in an unusual way." Dr. Azran looked perplexed.

"Who is responsible for maintenance and operation of your crematory system." Jeff frowned.

Number 1: The warranty is void and the causes seem to have been deliberate.

Number 2: Maximum allowable weight on the BLI-400 is 125 pounds. Automatic recordings show much greater weight has been used.

Number 3: The BLI-400 is capable of 850,000 BTU/hour. Someone electrically modified the motherboard to deliver twice the rated thermal power.

Number 4: Current specification is 10 amps. An improper modification increased that to 20 amperes; the wattage and resulting heat radiation were a dangerous combination.

Number 5: The rake that comes with the BLI-400 is meant to remove ashes, debris, metal rings or jewelry, titanium or metal body parts as well as bone fragments that must be raked out and mechanically pulverized. The failure to remove all remnants after cremation clearly initiated the massive power failure. Finding a wedding band and a silver crucifix should justify some explanation in a veterinary practice.

Number 6: This examination of bone fragments revealed an unusual and mysterious item that was identified as a human femur, one of the largest, human bones. The ID was done by the coroner.This finding was reported to certain legal entities. This will force a DNA analysis and potentially reveal a criminal act.

"Dr. Azran, there is no satisfaction in reporting such findings. I am sure the authorities will be visiting you to obtain more information such as who was in charge of cremations," Jeff continued, "Whoever did all the electronic modifications is damn good and could get a big job with L & N with no effort at all."

"Oh, my God, I can't even imagine what you have described, Jeff, "Gunter commented, "I don't even know what to say."

Dr. Azran stood silently in total amazement with his mouth open. His facial expression was a combination of shock, disbelief and a sense of horror.

Gunter grabbed chair that was near the door and helped Dr. Azran sit down.

"Are you alright, Harman?"

"Yes, of course, Gunter. Shocked? Yes. However, we must meet with L & N management to give us recommendations for a replacement."

CHAPTER 36

CORBIN SURFACES
IN LOS ANGELES

Escaping from Azran Clinic and leaving no means of tracing his whereabouts entailed rebuilding his curriculum vitae, his background or anything that would connect him to his past. He developed a chronological plan to change his entire life and leave no traces of any misdeeds real or imagined.

Corbin had opened an account with FaceBooks using an innocuous moniker. The profile he used was taken from the obituaries in the Los Angeles newspaper. Carson literally morphed into Ethan Levy, M.D. with the whisk of an ink pen and his criminal mentality.

Ego and bad judgment motivated him to contact Verna at Azran Clinic.

Dear Verna, You must forgive me for abandoning you and for the many mistakes I made with you. Replies to this communication are not possible presently. I came to the Los Angeles area intending to affiliate with Cedars-Sinai Medical Center. I applied for acceptance using the resume information of a Board Certified Internist who had died. You may contact me later under the name Ethan Levy. I successfully stimulated their interest and received a private call to a special number I had set up. I was living close to Glendale and the drive to Cedars-Sinai was not too far. I went to a personal interview with the Chief of Internal Medicine. Waiting in a large entry way, I spotted a doctor who I went to med school with. I knew he could recognize me and all my plans would be jeopardized. I knew my thoughts of being at Cedars-Sinai were impossible. Then, I contacted USC Verdugo Hills Hospital right here in Glendale. I googled the hospital and learned that all applicants had to get appointments through the head of Personnel and Human Relations whose name was Ariela Tannenbaum. I called her and announced myself as Ethan Levy. It worked and I was transferred to the head of internal medicine. We exchanged meaningless chit chat until he asked me to come in to meet him and be ready to go to work.

I have been doing some very private surgeries. I'm doing fifteen to twenty or more dilations and curettage procedures a week --- you remember, D and C, right. I know you would say that is risky, dangerous and illegal. However, I am a trained surgeon and each of these surgeries were done in sterile --- at least, sanitary conditions. Still way better than some midwife aborting with air embolisms or rusty coat hangers. Ten D & C procedures line my pockets with $6,000 per week. Since I started this the business, it has been bigger every month. When I am making closer to $300,000 a year, I will fly you wherever I happen to be. I realize, of course, the FDA is searching for me and you know the FBI is hot on my trail. You know, Verna, Covari was just an accident and he deserved what he got. I heard some rumors from people who knew and respected me. They said that I damaged the cremation machine and Azran was shut down because Covari's bones jammed the machine.

Never worry about that incident, Verna. You had nothing to do with disposing of Covari. It was entirely my decision and my action.

We had some good times, Verna. It is very unfortunate that circumstances prevented me from calibrating the audio oscillator that was implanted in your uterus. I wished that smooth, ELF would have been very soothing and enjoyable for you. A few minor adjustments would have made the extremely low frequencies a joy to your life.

I assure you that when you are with me, I will synchronize that oscillator to the ideal frequency.

I will contact you again soon. Please, do not share this communication with anyway and burn the copy preventing anyone looking for me from knowing where I might be.

Verna, the O.R. team here in Glendale Verdugo USC Hills Hospital is a tightly knit group of old friends and I get the cold shoulder from the nursing staff. It does get old.

A friend of mine from St. Louis contacts me periodically. I have not heard from him in over four years. Anyway, Verna, a letter from him caught up with me the day before yesterday. He is head of the physics department a Washington University. He tells me that if I am interested he can arrange a tenured position. He needs a scientific type guy to take over studies and research using analytical ultracentrifugation. He recalled that I had written technical papers on this subject. He says the position comes with full relocation expenses plus a great bonus. That bonus is --- listen to this --- the keys and deed to a classy home in Clayton. He assured me of an annual salary of $185,000 with an increase in six months to $200,000. He can plug me into the Barnes-Jewish Hospital complex and tells me that would provide another $150,000 to $200,000.

Yes, some risks would be inherent because there would be no AKA names. I would be back to plain Corbin Neeley. The total cash flow might make the risk of discovery of lesser concern.

I'm thinking about this very seriously.

"Verna, have you ever been to St. Louis?

There are many places to see in and around St. Louis. Way back in time, Verna, after my undergraduate studies, St. Louis Medical School made me a nice offer including a free, round-trip to look at the school. Anyway, Verna, I can show you a lot of things that I know you would enjoy. For instance, I remember that you really like candy. You loved any kind of licorice. Downtown St. Louis, very close to the Mississippi River, there is a place with more candy and ice cream sundaes than you have ever seen or imagined. It is called Crown Candies. You won't believe this but, I'm telling you that they have four different kinds of licorice and lots more from places in Europe.

Too, Verna, I want you to know how much I really care for you. I do know that there are rewards for any information leading to my arrest. I need you to trust me and understand that I will provide a comfortable and luxurious life style for you. I can set up bank accounts for you that will provide you far, far more money than the paltry rewards being offered.

Verna, if you ever cared for, even just a little, please do not share a shred of this information that I am telling you. Do, please, tear up any papers that you print, better yet run them through the shredder and burn them to ashes.

I will be setting up a computer system that will allow us to communicate with one another. I will program a code that only you and I will understand.

I do miss you, Verna. My next letter will probably be coming from St. Louis, Missouri.

CHAPTER 37

CARLTON IN KYOTO JAPAN

At the suggestion of Max Becker, Carlton planned a visit to Kyoto with intentions to establish an Objectives – Strategies-Methods Management system with Nihon Science.

His American Airlines miles had accumulated to over 65,000; his planned itinerary was to fly Japan Airlines and if possible fly first-class on a Being 777-777 which provided full bed convertibles in first-class. Upon arrival at Haneda Airport, a cab ride to central Tokyo where he could board the Shinkansen, the Bullet train to Nagoya. Carlton, at first, considered asking one of the employees at Nihon Science to pick him up in Nagoya. After, being advised by his computer that the drive would be some 90 miles one-way translating to over two hours of driving time or four hours plus just there and back, he revised his plan to the train.

Carlton's travel had focused on major cities, hospitals, and thermal services centers around the United States with periodic sales activities in the major cities in Canada. Carlton enjoyed places like Winnipeg, Vancouver, Montreal, and he was especially fond of Moose Jaw because it made him feel so continental.

Max's suggestion of flying to Japan on JAL, Japan Airlines, was an exciting concept and equally intriguing because he would be traveling on the Bullet train. He had practiced saying the word Shinkansen because it definitely made him feel like, at least, sound like a Bon Vivant. To adapt to his new feelings for things Japanese, he searched for genuine Japanese restaurants and was eating sushi or sashimi two or three times a week. Already, he had learned to order by simply asking for Omakase which he was taught by a

Nisei Japanese girl who told him that Omakase was asking the sushi chef to fix you the very freshest.

Carlton's itinerary had him flying JAL out of San Francisco with a brief stop in Honolulu. Then, Haneda airport in Tokyo. He would be spending a day or so in downtown Tokyo before taking the Shinkansen to Nagoya where he might change trains to Osaka at the suggestion of Max Becker. His plan was to take a train from Osaka after a few days and be in Kyoto to speak with Hideo Yamaguchi, the Chief Operating Officer of Nihon Science which was a subsidiary of Gigatrax, the holding company. Carlton had memorized a Japanese expression spoken as 'Summi Masen', literally translated as close as possible to "sorry, excuse me."

Carlton spent a single day dazed by the complexity of Tokyo traffic and the vast variety of noodles for sale right on the streets. He quickly adapted to looking at the plastic replicas of food in restaurant windows.

Japanese children using the Shinkansen were a fascination to Carlton. They were all dressed in school uniforms and acted with perfect manners and polite decorum.

Calton succumbed to a Bento box sales person and opted for the sales person's suggestion for innari. Carlton had no idea of what he might get to eat. The rice ball in a Tofu bag surprised him and he waited until the sales person came around again and he ordered more of the same.

As the train moved at high speeds in a Southerly direction, he noticed people looking out the windows on the right side. He recognized Mt. Fuji and took a series of photos.

Carlton was developing nostalgia for his favorite things back home in California. He was already feeling that any extended time in Japan wouldn't be in his best interest. He had suspicions even premonitions that the decreasing profitability from the Japanese subsidiary would continue unless some important changes were made before the next quarter. Carlton had reviewed all the quarterly Income Statements from Nihon Sciences and compared the performance to other subsidiaries of Gigatrax. There was no requirement for a statistical genius, a CPA, or a mind reader; it was apparent as the whiskers on his chin that problems at Nihon Science were rampant.

With all the analytical factors considered, Carlton developed a deepening concern as to why Max had not discussed Japan's performance with him. He knew that Max was an astute CEO. He felt his own selling abilities were certainly superior to Max's. When he considered analytical acumen, he felt Max had the edge on him.

With all his cogitation, he questioned why Max suggested this trip to

Nihon Science with no remarks of expectations, instructions or recommended actions.

Carlton mental activities were jumbled by the unusual sounds of the Shinkansen. Stark realization that he was in Japan, on the Bullet train, headed to Kyoto and would be meeting with Hideo Yamaguchi turned on the light bulbs.

"Wow, Damn, why didn't I see this coming. I'm out here in left field and couldn't even see the ball coming."

Carlton thought about calling Max right now until he remembered that the time was something else back home. Too, he looked at all the people with cell phones on the train but noticed that no one was talking on the phone at all. His texting skill was nil. He didn't like texts and never bothered.

His thoughts returned to business and this troubling matter about Nihon Science. "Okay," he mumbled, "Max may be transferring me to Kyoto to run Nihon Science. Then, he may be thinking about putting my ass out to pasture." Carlton's eyes widened and he scanned all the Japanese faces on the train.

Carlton started introspection regarding his executive position in Gigatrax. Again, he lip synced, "Consider who would run Biotherm with me in Kyoto"? At that precise moment, Carlton decided to change his entire itinerary. He would forget Osaka. Another train from Nagoya could get him to Kyoto much faster. He decided he would reaffirm his management skills by contacting Max from Kyoto and tell Max that he wants to terminate Hideo Yamaguchi.

Carlton deliberated about his planned action with the Senior Executive at Nihon Science. After all, he thought, why would anyone with a name that practically translated Yamaguchi to Big Mouth get to be a senior executive. Carlton shook his head to clear the imaginary cobwebs.

Carlton spoke out loud, "Get back to reality, Herrick. Shut up and get with it. Now, get the train from Nagoya to Kyoto, contact Yamaguchi with my itinerary and ask him to meet me at the train station and plan dinner together someplace in Kyoto and, yes, make me reservations for three nights at a comfortable but economical Japanese spa."

Weather in Kyoto was spectacular. The trip from Nagoya was uneventful confirming Carlton's decision to alter his itinerary. Carlton and a large group of traveling Japanese people were released into the main terminal. Carton was easily recognized, a well-attired Japanese man had spotted him and was waving his hand holding a paper sign reading Mr. Herrick.

Hideo Yamaguchi kept bowing as Carlton approached him. Carlton extended his handshake which Hideo returned with a combination bow and weak handshake.

"Hello, Mr. Herrick, I am Hideo Yamaguchi. Please call me Hide."

"Oh, Hide, please call me Carlton," Carlton bent slightly from the waist, "konichi wa."

"You speak Japanese?" Hideo appeared surprised.

"No, I picked up a few words. No, I don't know Japanese but I love Japanese food."

"Very good, Carltonsan, I have arranged dinner where you will be staying. The Nishiyama Ryokan is Ichiban with much Japanese culture. Staff speaks English and guests may keep shoes on." Hideo explained.

"Good, Hide, I want to be in the office in the morning. What time will I be picked up?"

"I will pick you up, Carltonsan. A plant tour will be available by ten o'clock if acceptable to you."

"Hide," Carlton spoke as he consulted his Japanese-English pamphlet, "Doho desu ka?"

Hide clapped his hands twice saying, "Perfect, Carltonsan. It is close here in Kyoto only a few minutes walk from train station here. I have arranged a special meal there. I am hoping you enjoy fish."

"I like sashimi very much. Natto? No, I can't take the smell, Hide."

"Neither can I, Carltonsan. Ready? My car is close by. We can go if you are ready."

Carlton was favorably impressed with the Nishiyama Ryokan. His room was not typically Japanese.

It was not Tatami floor with an uncomfortable mat on the floor which he had worried about.

He and Carlton sampled various types of sake at the hotel cocktail lounge before going to dinner.

After several cold Sake drinks, Carlton had a question, "Hide, we can talk business tomorrow. I do want to ask you one or two questions."

"Yes, Carltonsan, please continue," Hide answered as he spilled his sake cup, "what can I tell you?"

"As the senior executive at Nihon Science, Hide, how frequently do you review the Balance Sheet and Income Statement?"

"I discuss financials with accounting department sometimes." Hide squirmed and poured more sake into Carlton's cup.

"And, Hide, how often do you meet with all department heads?"

"Most every month except that the head of operations does not live near

Kyoto, but I talk with him quarterly. If you have other questions, I will need my staff around the table for good answers." Hide attempted to refill Carlton's sake cup that was already filled. He over poured sake onto the table.

"Hide, are you aware that Nihon Science monthly expense for the last nine months have been growing and exceeding gross income by a factor of two?" Carlton turned his sake cup upside down indicating he was finished drinking.

"As I said, Caroltonsan, my staff can answer all your questions in the morning before lunch." Hide's left eye started twitching.

Carlton's mind went in silent meditation with an immediate conclusion. Before he said another word, he asked himself a single question. "Why or for what value would I stay here another day or two? The problem is as easy to see as my SIU class ring right here on my right hand."

Dinner was preplanned. Yamaguchi had discussed selections directly with a master sushi chef who had spent two years exclusively on rice preparation. Yamaguchi had requested that Blue Fin Maguro be available. He was extensively experienced in the handling and preparation of various ocean fish. He insisted on the most delicious part of the Tuna which he stipulated must be either haranaki, chutoro or harakami, the fattest section of the Tuna.

"Hide, summimasen, the sake is making me feel ill. I must pass on dinner. I am sorry. I must go to bed."

Carlton and Hide Yamaguchi parted after Carlton said: "See you here in the morning."

Carton relaxed in his room making notes of his observations and comments made earlier. He felt flabbergasted that this grievous financial fiasco could have continued this long. He had laid out his report in a classical Balance Sheet format.

The last line underlined was "Total restructure of Nihon Science" vital immediately.

Before going to bed for a well-earned sleep, he decided to make a private call to Max and discuss his plan of action.

CHAPTER 38

CORBIN AT BARNES HOSPITAL IN ST. LOUIS

Corbin had thought a long time about his offer from his friend in St. Louis. He found little if any ego satisfaction from his surgical assignments at Verdugo Hills and nothing was exciting or intriguing about living in Glendale. His casual acquaintances in the hospital would painfully listen to his complaints about the city. Without exception, his villifying tirade was countered with some form of the same question which was "Gee, Dr. Neeley, you should just wait until you see the New Year's Day Parade." Corbin's characteristically jocular responses were either, "I'd rather watch paint dry", or "I'd prefer to do crossword puzzles".

When Corbin finished his pre-medical studies, he optimistically applied to Harvard Medical Med school, Stanford Med school, Louisiana State, MIT, University of Illinois plus Tulane and his backup choice, St. Louis Medical school.

He received initially favorable interest from St.Louis, Tulane, and the University of Illinois. Conversely, he got standard, gobbledegook boilerplate from Harvard and Stanford. St. Louis University Medical school made a magnanimous offer to pay first class, roundtrip airfares plus a teaching assistantship for $1500 monthly.

The St. Louis offer was intriguing with some cash flow attractions. He decided to accept that offer for an interview.

Corbin laid out a strategic plan to meet his objective if he decided in favor of St. Louis. These plans included a paddle boat trip down the Mississippi to New Orleans which might fit his interest in Tulane and LSU. The St. Louis

Gateway Arch was included in his places to see. Uniquely, a visit to Crowns Candy and Ice Cream Parlor was a must to visit for his sweet tooth. Corbin had been given good advice to spend time in an area called the Hill. A friend told him it was the best Italian food anywhere. His friend called that section of St. Louis, "Dago Hill" which Corbin questioned, "Did you say Dago Hill?" His friend answered, "I did say Dago Hill cause I live there and, by the way, did you forget my name is Appino? You recall that I was an Italian long before I was a doctor, recall? Shaw's Botanical Gardens is noted as a place to use your camera."

Corbin promised himself way back then that the sights and personal interests would not sway his decision to St. Louis Medical school. However, the situation today was a totally different situation. Without any question, Corbin was ready to leave California. True, he knew that St. Louis Winters were not warm, sunny beach weather and mid-Summer is St. Louis can be sweltering hot with matching high humidity.

The cash flow and the prestigious home in Clayton and the opportunity to reestablish his reputation as a professional physician and surgeon were all strong motivators. Too, his affiliation with the Physics Department at Washington University was strongly appealing. There with university funding, grants, and Angel investments, he could possibly further develop his ideas for using low-frequency as well as ultra-high frequency sounds to resolve medical malfunctions.

Corbin after due deliberation decided to take the St. Louis opportunity. He contacted banks in and around Clayton to establish credit lines and determine property values. After locating, the most aggressive and successful real estate brokers in Clayton, He put the home that was gifted to him up for sale on a net mortgage expecting a bottom line profit of $800,000. He arranged a rental home in the Italian section of St. Louis known as "The Hill".

He established a medical practice on the Hill as an obstetrics and gynecology specialist. He started low visibility advertising to control undesired pregnancy. Well before the first patients inquired, he was deluged with investment seekers fascinated with the control of pregnancy. Nothing related to loss of embryo or life or death, but the dominant financial motivation was to bilk pregnant females who could pay his $10,000 D and C fee.

Corbin had a peculiar attraction akin to a fetish of the Soulard area of St. Louis. He located a "watering hole" of sound reputation named The International Tap House. He had developed the habit of going here several times a week and had learned to appreciate the tastes of many of the beers available there.

His motivation stemmed from his intention to construct or rebuild a private office with a small surgical suite. He had become quite accustomed to being called an abortionist as well as many other unsavory names. The word names should bring to mind the expression "Sticks and stones may break my bones, but words will never hurt me". This was the precise code that Corbin adopted.

At Washington University, he was simply Dr. Neeley and highly regarded as a talented physical chemist and expert with analytical ultracentrifugation skills. His reputation as a teaching professor had attracted Master's Degree candidates from numerous other schools around the country.

The Barnes-Jewish Complex had established his reputation as one of the most skilled gastroenterologists in St. Louis if not the entire country. In a very brief amount of time, over 80% of gastric surgeries or interventions were done by Dr. Neeley.

In Soulard, he was Corbin and called "Doc" by anyway who frequented the International Tap House. He had made it known that he intended to build, construct or reconstruct his new, private office and surgical suites right here in Soulard and his favorite place was close to this building he was visiting with such regularity. He also made impressions with his willingness to buy drinks for everyone at the bar.

His practiced ability to talk with anyone and everyone spread the word that this doctor was performing doctor-assisted abortions to unwed females and allowing the needy to pay his fees in small installments. Corbin had decided that Soulard was the ideal locations for a private office that offered obstetrical and gynecological procedures. His plan included bringing in a fresh ob/gyn specialist with exciting 401(k) plans that might allow him to relocate or more simply to run and continue hiding from arrest and prison.

Corbin's continual fear of being recognized forced him to modify his appearance, his manner of dress and his hair style. He had met with surgeons involved with plastic surgery who introduced him to Sonobello. At one of the Sonobello locations, he negotiated complete alterations of his facial feature in exchange for surgical assistance in belly and body fat procedures.

He made it a habit, a poor one, to visit Crown Candy whenever the notice struck him. A street musician playing kettle drum always kept his attention. In some way, the musician began calling him doc. I t bothered Corbin a bit. After several weeks, the musician asked "doc" if he could help him with a "young girl's problem".

This, then, was the beginning of a continuing relationship between these two opportunists. Corbin increased these D & C procedures in the areas around Crown's Candy using an ambulance he had rented and modified with capabilities such as irrigation, aspiration and basic anesthesia as needed.

This continued much longer than Corbin had expected. After some three or four months, the Musician contacted Corbin advising him that a St. Louis uniformed, police officer was asking him about someone driving in this area and routinely parking on Mallinckrodt St. Corbin instructed his friend to just clam up and tell the cop that you never saw any ambulance around Crown Candy.

One week later around nine in the evening, Corbin drove over to the International Tap House with a taste for a nice cold Pilsner. Parking next door to his favorite bar was rarely if ever a problem. He headed into his customary street parking spot glancing down 9th St. And noticing a St. Louis black and white. He was not gravely surprised or concerned with any cops in or around Soulard.

Corbin was already tasting that cold Pilsner as he opened the door and started to walk right in. Standing at the bar, he saw the driver of the black and white on the street. Nobody had seen him coming in.

Flight or fight was his next thought. He wisely opted for flight.

Within the next two minutes, he realized his job at Washington University was finished. He would make no effort to tell friends and associates at Barnes-Jewish goodbye. His private office and surgical suites that he had longed thought about were abruptly gone. Saying goodbye to some beer drinking pals there in The International Tap House --- no way.

CHAPTER 39

ATTRITION HITS BIOTHERM

The semiconductor market and the careers of executives in the business skyrocketed in the early days of .com. It was beyond imagination.

The market was fragmented into small, new .com operations with hungry appetites for more gifted and ingenious electronic engineers with unique abilities to compress more and more circuits on smaller and smaller breadboards and converting them to silicon chips or newer substrates.

Semiconductor growth and the expanding markets and submarkets created an explosion of personal income, fringes, and perquisites for those individuals that took responsibility for the ballooning market demand. In many of the new semiconductor companies, the company culture rapidly transmogrified to engineering and high technology and high-risk investments.

Migration between semiconductor companies was a modus operandi. Engineers who had been earning usual annual salaries encountered a solid gold opportunity to earn and be paid well in excess of $100,000 or more. It was commonly assumed that all semiconductor employees were extremely wealthy. The Silicon Valley real estate market increased the sales price of the everyday three bedrooms, two bath homes in Cupertino, Santa Clara and surroundings from prices as low as $12,000 up to over $300,000 and higher and growing fast.

The vast number of executives outside of the semiconductor business made substantially less than rank and file semiconductor employees. Gradual price increases forced lower income individuals to seek other employment and, in some cases, relocate away from Silicon Valley.

Poaching of employees began slowly but grew in grand style. As home prices escalated, recruiting well-educated candidates from the Midwest or the Eastern Seaboard was cramping the style of free spending, company recruiters. The solution to offer big money bonuses for accepting employment plus providing nice homes in nice areas with the mortgage paid by the recruiting company appeared to resolve such aggravations.

The outgoing cash flow begged for better accounting and financial systems. The stark realization of inept management at the financial level hit hard. Basic financial management ratios were completely alien to college graduates with high technology, electronic degrees.

Death of the .com slapped lots of faces. However, market demands still grew in log scale. Semiconductor growth demanded continuous cash flow. Financial sense was finally the savior of may IT companies.

Gigatrax lived day to day with Income Statements and Balance Sheets and religious fervor for financial ratios on every subsidiary and every department within each subsidiary.

The flow of e-mails, memos and statistical date hitting Max Becker's desk daily was enormous.

K. B. Randall as Vice-President and Chief Financial Office for Gigatrax had hired Eilene Barton to manage control all accounting activities and to statically analyze any data relating to money in or money out. Eilene was a Ph.D. graduate in Finance with a parallel degree in Statistical analysis from Wharton School of Business. Eilene was a CPA gifted in numerical manipulations.

She buzzed K. B. Randall and requested time to discuss what she described as critical dangers requiring immediate intervention.

"Eilene, you know my door is always open, come on up --- right now if you want to talk eye ball to eye ball, okay?"

"This is every bit that important. I'll be there in five." Eilene spoke with urgency.

In well under five minutes, Eilene was in front of K. B. desk. "Sit down, Eilene." K.B. pointed at a chair.

Still standing, Eilene began her concerns. "I need to say this first, K. B., okay? Each management faux pas I explain is not of itself catastrophic. However, the synergy between just the first four need your attention."

"Fine, Eilene, go ahead, relax and begin," what has caused you to be so upset?"

"Turmoil at the Board of Directors level is not on my list of assignments. Rumors are floating on the floor that the subsidiary companies are eroding the financial strength of Gigatrax."

"I hear you, Eilene. Continue, we can talk later." K. B. had a thick frown across her forehead.

"I never lie to apologize for being a statistical nut. Well, statistics never lie but statisticians do."

"Yes, I know, you told me that before. Eilene. Please, go ahead,"

"The performance of Nihon Science is beyond an abomination. For the last four quarters, Japanese pricing of Gigatrax products is going to initiate a Congressional investigation if not worse."

"I have the same concern about Nihon Science. Their financials read like pure fabrications. Spending has gone three sigmas and to the right. Three standard deviations can be a loud scream. It is not necessary to recalculate the normal curve."

"I'm understanding every point that you make, Eilene. Let me have your bottom line."

"Why is nothing being done to stop the drain on our company. I mean, our year end financials are consolidated and Nihon Science is the culprit, J. B. I know you understand."

"I more than understand. You are describing a grave and dangerous situation. Are you ready to go to Max Becker and let him hear your findings?"

"Absolutely, J. B., I will do my best to maintain my decorum when I talk to the big Boss."

K. B. and Eilene contacted Max Becker and asked, "This is K. B. and I would like to meet soon as possible with Eilene Barton to give you some very disquieting information that Eilene has reported."

"Come on down, both of you. I'm sitting here anxious to hear what Eilene has learned."

K. B. said, "Max is a good listener, Eilene. So do not hold back. Let him have the data you discussed with me and don't worry about anything, okay?"

The meeting in Max's office was essentially a repeat of everything Eilene had reported to K. B. excepting the frightening attrition of long time Biotherm employees.

Max listened carefully. Hearing about the losses of Biotherm, he stood up from his desk.

"Eilene, have you made a report about this attrition problem. It hurts me hearing that good employees are leaving."

"Yes, sir, "K. B. interjected," the newer dot com companies are proselytizing people with big salary increases, promises of bonuses, financial help with home mortgages, and things beyond imagination."

"I had heard comments that the Peninsula Human Relations Group was working inter-company to stop that practice," Max was grinding his teeth, "K.B., will you and Eilene develop a substantiating report for my review. You are guaranteed that corrections will be made.

CHAPTER 40

REORGANIZATION OF GIGATRAX

Max Becker was visually agitated enough to bite galvanized nails. He liked and respected K. B. and he felt Elaine was one of the brightest statisticians he had ever worked with. His hatred of stupid errors and repeating mistakes increased his blood pressure and decreased his ability to curtail his bad language.

Max's Intel phone contained a database that was programmed with names categorized by occupation, age, zip codes, his own evaluation code for the confidence level, favorite dessert, meat or vegetable eater, religious leanings, motivations, favorite drink, alcoholic usage, estimated net worth and other details on people near or associated with him. Max guarded this confidential data with the mentality of a German Police dog and he had insured the privacy of the data with Lloyd's of London.

Using this capability, contacting all the present Board Members simultaneously was kindergarten play.

Max first made penciled notes of his intent. Then, after due diligence and in-depth concentration on precisely what he was about to say to all board members it was saved to his private communication file.

His communication was directed to Jim Calder, James DeVue, Ken Elwood, Kenny McMasters. He modified the recipient's list excluding both K. B. and Carlton.

The message was succinct and clear:

GENTLEMEN, Two days away, dramatic changes will be presented to the Board. It is critically important that we all meet in the Gigatrax Conference Room Thursday at 1930 precisely. Bonus payable for attendees.

Max Becker felt deluged with too much information of problems that had the potential to do serious damage to the plan for Gigatrax. Too any Board Members were grumbling about unrest at Biotherm. The attrition was increasing which included loss of some key people. This bothered Max because a problem such as this was not brought to his attention. Certainly, it meant that someone was not doing their job properly. The Board was questioning the very concept of subsidiary companies. Hourly workers had joined together under the Biotherm banner criticizing the decision to remove Clarence Harwood from the Board. These rumors peeved Max because he had always held an unvoiced belief which was 'Never let the inmates run the asylum'.

More recently, a telephone cal from Carlton caught him off guard. Carlton described a grim financial picture and described what he called a total lack of control at Nihon Science. Carlton wanted hm to sanction the decision to terminate Hideo Yamguchi. Of greater significance, Carlton had totally disregarded his suggestions to go to Osaka before Kyoto.

Before discussion with the Board, Max decided to call Carlton in the evening about nine or ten at the hotel number that Carlton had given him.

Max's call was handled by an International Operator and Carlton was on the line within minutes.

"Hello, Max, this is Carlton, of course. You up early, Max?"

"I want you to listen first. We can talk later. These instructions I will give you are not suggestions, Carlton."

"Okay, Max. I am listening."

"First, do not fire Yamaguchi. You know Japan. A firing to a Japanese person is a complete loss of face.

So, Carlton, move him to a job where he can't do any damage. Remove him from all distribution lists. The Japanese call this and I am quoting 'Seat by the window", Max sounded angry, "managing international employees is alien to selling, Carlton."

"Yes,sir, I understand what you are saying, "Carlton tried his most contrite voice.

"No, Carlton, you went to Nihon Science because I already knew a problem existed. I fully expected you to detect it in short order. I further expected you to separate the problems minor and major. I mean in a statistical array from major significance down to simply minor ---"

"Yes, Max, pretty much what I did. Yamaguchi is the apex of the problems."

"Carlton, selecting a culprit for assigning all blame is not management. It is a cheap way to escape responsibility."

"Tell me this, Max," Carlton waffled, "did you send me to Nihon Science expecting me to fail so you could call and chew my ass out?"

"I am expecting you to demonstrate your executive abilities which you are not showing with problems you have identified, but have not detailed to your own satisfaction much less to mine."

"What do you want me to do, Max. Am I next in line for out the door?"

"To the opposite extreme. So, make notes of what I am insisting upon, understand?"

"I'm writing --- go ahead."

"First, Carlton, remain in Japan. Introduce yourself as a business consultant as you take full command of Nihon Science. This will not resolve all problems that have mushroomed to company killers. I expect you to be in Kyoto, probably two years, move your family at company expense. That decision must be yours."

"How can I manage Biotherm living in Japan, Max?"

"Biotherm has a set of independent problems that were not of your doing, but they were slipping right by you."

"Is this your way of asking for my resignation, Max?"

"As I explained before. This is vital to get Gigatrax back on course and provide you an invaluable experience to turn Nihon Science into a prosperous, successful operation."

"You have hit me with a big thing to think about. How will you manage Biotherm, Max?"

"This week, I am naming K. B. as President and C.O.O of Biotherm."

"Ooh, Max, you really know how to hurt a guy."

"Not my reason for these actions. We will talk very personally when we are across the desk from each other."

"If you choose to remain as CEO with K.B. reporting to you, that is acceptable. Your net worth will take a dramatic upsweep, Carlton. We will discuss in private. Yes, I gave you a lot to ponder about. I expect your favorable decisions in the next day."

CHAPTER 41

CORBIN IN NEW ORLEANS

The flight from Lambert Field Airport in St. Louis to Louis Armstrong Airport in New Orleans changed altitudes often attempting to avoid the rough and uncomfortable conditions. The turbulence and instances of negative gravity had floated several pieces of small bags and a laptop computer or two. The seat belt signs had been on since the flight took off. Announcements had been made regularly encouraging passengers to remain seated and keep their seat belts attached. The Flight Attendants had challenges helping passengers who needed help.

One elderly man removed his seat belt and headed down the aisle toward the lavatory. The airplane shifted and the man fell sideways hitting his head on the arm of a seat. When he failed to get back up, two flight attendants rushed to help him get back into a seat and hook up his seat belt. He was not bleeding and appeared to be alright.

The pilot had selected another altitude and the plane regained a smooth and comfortable ride.

A middle-aged man sitting next to Corbin had pestered the flight attendant time and time again to bring him another champagne. His drinking had become overly excessive and with each successive bottle of champagne, his grabbing at the attendant's private areas became well beyond excessive. Carlton aggravated with his fellow passenger's behavior and was making signals to the attendant to stop giving him liquor.

The attendant picked up on Corbin's signals and talked with one of the other Flight Attendants.

"Honey," she said, "I have an already inebriated ass with his hands all over me and demanding another drink. His seat mate has had enough and is getting irritated."

"Well, enough is enough, girl. Let me handle the matter."

The problem-solving attendant located a warm bottle of champagne but decided to substitute a pink Rose champagne. She sauntered provocatively down the aisle approaching the drunk."

Yes, sir, you wanted another bottle of champagne, correct? I brought one for you."

"Yeah, put it on my tray here but open it first, cutie., he blabbered.

She held the champagne bottle in front of his face close to his ear as she snapped off the cap. Most of the liquid spewed out onto his face and wet his shirt completely.

He shouted at her, "You stupid bitch!"

Corbin was drinking a cup of coffee. He turned and sloshed the full cup of hot coffee directly on the man's pants.

The pilot, Captain of the plane was there immediately and took command of the problem speaking right in the face of the yelling passenger.

"Sir, I will call ahead and have police ready to arrest you. Sit there and shut up or else."

Applause was heard from several adjacent passengers.

After landing, the Captain had kept his promise. Two airport policemen came on the plane and escorted the champagne drinker into a waiting police vehicle.

Corbin held his breath as long as the policemen were on the plane. He waited until all the passengers were getting off and saw the police car drive away.

The two Flight Attendants both gave his high fives and kissed him on the cheek. They both congratulated him on his behavior on their behalf.

His first shock after walking toward the baggage area was the heat. He began sweating and thinking about renting a car with good air conditioning. He realized that he had failed to make reservations anywhere. He decided to go directly to the French Quarter and search out a room or some place with great air conditioning.

By sheer happnstance, he bumped into the two, good-looking Flight Attendants that had spoken with him on the plane.

"Excuse me, ladies," he said, "are you laying over here in New Orleans?"

"Yes, we are. Do you live here in NOLA?"

"I will be soon. I need to decide to look for a place to live. Can you give me any suggestions?"

On of the attendants spoke up, "I think we owe you that much. You helpd out nice on the plane."

The other attendant placed her hand on Corbin's shoulder. "We are staying at the Marriott in the Quarter. Give me a call and we can meet, have a cold drink and give you our suggestions"

She handed a pencilled note with her name.

Corbin thanked them saying "I'll see if I can get a room at the Marriott."

"Great, by the way, what is your name?"

The other girl said, "What do you do anyway?"

Corbin decided not to use his real name. He answered, "I'm a doctor."

"Thanks again. See you in the Marriott, doctor."

CHAPTER 42

CORBIN RECRUITS PARTNER IN FRENCH QUARTER

If you had committed a crime and All Points Bullets indicated that you were getting higher and higher on the wanted list, fear of capture and punishment would be significant on your list of concerns. If you wanted to hide being in New Orleans might not be your best decision. A poor decision, of course, is continuing illegal, immoral or illicit activities. Your decision to hide out and increase illegal and/or immoral activities in the French Quarter is close to your worst thought. Bourbon Street is dense with party people all year around. During Mardi Gras, Bourbon Street is unquestioningly the worst plan to violate laws, Local, State, Federal, or any other infringements.

Corbin Neeley made all of these worst decisions including personal habits. Bad habits and his decisions had denigrated to dealing pot, oxycodone, Percocet, injected mushrooms and most any gender prostitution. He used his forged and illegal medical credentials under the Ethan Levy, M.D.

All of Ethan Levy's credentials verified his degree in medicine from Ben Gurion University in Israel including his identification as his Jewish background.

Using his years of deception, dishonesty, and outright lies, Corben had degraded his reputation totally. His past accomplishments, his relationships as well as his future were history. Corbin --- that is Dr. Ethan Levy had established a friend and drinking buddy who listened to all of the sordid events of Corbin's --- Ethan Levy's past. Dr. Levy had established the habit of keeping open tabs at most of the bars and burlesque places on Bourbon Street. His friend, Jason Gormley, explained that he was an ex-cotton picker and truck driver living on a pittance and readily allowing Dr. Levy to pick up the tab wherever they drank. Jason Gormley became a friend, philosopher, and counselor to Ethan.

Ethan invites his friend, Jason to partake of the available easy money in and around NOLA. Ethan asked, "Jason, I have plenty of money and lots of my income is from other sources than medical practices. You are one of my few real friends here in Louisiana; the one shortcoming I have is just available time."

"Well, doc, if I could help you in any way, you know I would, but I'm not sure how to help."

"Well, Jason, your periodic counseling is more help than you can imagine. Answer a question for me, okay?"

"You bet, doc, what question you got? Jason asked quizzically.

"Easy one, Jason. Tell me, if you will, what do you think of me --- really?"

"Not easy for me, doc. You sure you want me pickin' at your bones?"

"That is why I asked, my friend. Go ahead, fire away!"

"Doc, don't want to hurt your feelings, but to me you have swerved way off course from an unbelievable professional career like practicing medicine and surgery on both people and animals in California, Missouri and now Louisiana. To me, it makes me kind of sorry."

"Jason, I want to hear what you are thinking about. Don't even think of hurting my feelings" This declaration came with a pat on the shoulder.

"Doc, better get us another cold one now. After, you may kick my ass out of here. Anyway, your ups and downs in life look like nothing to look backward to with pride and nothing to look forward to with hope."

"Wow, Jason, I heard that before. Do I seem that pitiful?"

Jason picked up his cold glass of beer and seemed to contemplate before deciding what he wanted to say.

"Doc, we have spent lots of time together. I know you ain't the straight arrow guy that people see."

"Meaning what?", Ethan queried.

"You have explained a whole lot to me about your past. Sometimes over way too much hooch, you have revealed way more than you probably remember.", Jason opened the discussion further, "Too, Doc, this is the computer age and even I can google all kinds of info with relative ease."

"Surprisingly, Jason, I have no discomfort with that. In fact, it relates precisely to how you can, indeed, help me.

This remark did surprise even shock Jason. "Doc, I hear rumblings from the French Quarter that the New Orleans police have allegations of your involvement in human trafficking."

"Rumors are like sticks and stones, they don't hurt anyone, Jason. Bottom line, Jason, would you consider working with me --- knowing the risk, but able to pocket over ten thousand dollars under the table each month." Ethan picked up his glass of beer and held it up to toast the conversation, "seriously, Jason."

"Seriously, Doc, guess if we are forming a partnership, I can just call you Ethan, Okay?"

"No, not quite yet, Jason. We need to talk in much more detail before you jump into something you really don't know. It is vital that you know and understand the downside risks of being involved with me in any kind of matter."

"Yes, I do agree with your thinking. Frankly, you have only known me for a few short weeks and as it is, you know effectively nothing. As you have clearly explained the risks, you need to better understand the risks of being involved with me."

"Touche!," Ethan added, "you have never been involved in anything clandestine in your life. As a cotton picker, what was the biggest trouble you ever encountered."

"And ---," Ethan interjected, "as a truck driver."

"It is about things about me that you just don't know," Jason warned.

"We have established a working partnership. Anything one partner does directly or indirectly affects the other partner or, for that matter, partners. Am I clear on that point?" Ethan's facial expression indicated anger.

"You made your point. You college guys always want to set the tone and progress of every event and it appears that you want total control of relationships as well, is that right?" Jason tried to make his point.

"Let me put it this way, partner. If there is something about you that puts me at risk, I need to know specific details. In other words, if you observe me making a critical mistake, I expect you to set me straight and I mean before anything else happens."

"Look, doc, I understand what you say about the partnership, but you need to understand that I am not joining your fraternity. Conversely, to your comments, I do not want to be liable for mistakes you make. Do you accept my philosophical view."

"I will say this, Jason, we must trust each other for any partnership relationship to function well."

CHAPTER 43

CORBIN ARRESTED IN FRENCH QUARTER

Jason Gormley has agreed to meet Corbin (aka Ethan Levy) in a well-known club on Bourbon Street called the NOLA NUDES GENTLEMAN'S CLUB. Both men had previously discussed a working partnership with promises to Jason Gormley of lots of cash flow. There were two innuendoes that they had agreed to evaluate and meet at NOLA NUDES to discuss details such as more info on cash flow and another matter of how and where payments for illegal activities would be handled.

Dr. Levy had walked all the way to the Gentlemen's Club from Esplanade to 420 Bourbon Street. He was a regular at the club and was recognized immediately by two barkers at the door touting bottomless girls, cold beer, and genuine real Absinthe. Dr. Levy nodded to them and explained that he was expecting a good friend in a few minutes.

Dr. Levy exchanged a fist handshake with both men saying, "I will have the cash for you both later."

Repeating their handshakes, they both said, "Welcome, Doc, we got a few new young ones lined up for you.

Ethan walked through a small crowd looking for a quiet, secluded table.

Three attractive women dressed in varying degrees of nudity approached Ethan's table. Ethan welcomed each of them by name, "Janie, is that drink in your hand for me?" She set the drink in front of Ethan along with an envelope marked $1,480. Ethan nodded his appreciation, "Nice work, Janie. Your commissions will be available in three days in your account."

"Take a look at my envelope, doc." The statuesque blond handed her larger envelope to Ethan. He noted the scribbled pencil mark as $7,655. "Very good work, Ruth. This will likely win the bonus this week."

The third girl appeared much too young to be called a woman. She blurted out her remark before Ethan had finished his last remark, "Doc, I'll bet you $1,000 that I will earn this week's bonus. Check my figures here."

On the envelope, Ethan now held, he read aloud very slowly "Damn, Curry, fifteen thousand and six-hundred dollars, wow! Now scoot, girls, I am expecting company, but before you leave, do have some drinks at the bar. Use my tab."

"Thanks, doc, we spotted three Johns at the bar sloshing down martinis and beer chasers. They should be ready to party by now".

Still awaiting Jason's arrival, Ethan checked his suit coat pockets counting the number of small, plastic bags of Apple Jacks and the number of cigar tubes disguising tightly rolled Bonanos. In Ethan's coat sleeve pocket, he had secured four or five packs of Aunt Hazel. His best calculation was that he was a walking drug shop with somewhere close to $85,000 to $90,000 at street value.

After all his preparation, he reached for the drink left by one of the hustlers --- he couldn't remember her name. He never remembered names but never forgot who owed him or what they had promised. He studied the lipstick smudges around the lip of the glass and felt revulsion of the girl. As a trained doctor, dirt and filth were abhorrent to him. As a drug merchant and a rich, successful pimp, his whole personality had deteriorated to just another piece of migrating French Quarter trash.

Corbin had never smoked. He had always avoided alcohol or any artificially stimulating substance. Today, after a not too distant past, he had grown and sold every possible form of cannabis --- strictly wholesale. His badly mistaken idea was that if he sold only to distributors and never to sell to drunks or high users, his crime would be minor and not punishable. Such thinking from an individual with advanced learning and professional degrees is well beyond understanding. He kept copious records of all the people, clubs, distributors, and agencies who had ever purchased or dealt with him.

Curry, the girl whose envelope contained over fifteen thousand dollars returned to Dr. Levy's table.

"Sit down, kid," he said, "what is on your mind?"

"Come on, Doc, how come you call me kid anyway?"

"Well, how come they call you Curry?"

"Easy, Doc," she cooed, "I used to work at the race track at Santa Anita. I curry combed horses."

"Alright, kid, I know you didn't come over here for a rap session. So, say what you were gonna' say."

"Okay, doc, I thank you for all the money going into my account. I owe you more than just thanks."

"No thanks required, kid."

"I know, doc, but you do not make it with any of the girls. I know, you don't sleep with anyone."

"Getting a bit personal, Curry?"

"Yes, doc, as a matter of fact, yes --- in fact, yes. I am a sixteen-year-old kid, but I have noticed that you like my ass and watch me when I walk."

"Back off now, kid," he interrupted, "I am not one of your johns."

"I'd like it," she answered, "when did you have any young stuff last, doc? I promise you never had any this good," she said as she leaned into his arm on the table, "would you like a taste?"

"You want to do something here at the table". He growled.

"If you want, doc," she said as she unbuttoned her blouse exposing her breasts.

"One more mistake like you are about to take and you will never see another cent from me in your account. So, get out of my face and never try this kind of action with me ever again."

As Curry walked away, he observed someone entering as sunlight illuminated the entry way. Momentarily unable to focus, Corbin held his hand in front of his eyes. As his eyes adjusted, he recognized Jason Gormley approaching his table.

Within a few yards of reaching the table, Corbin watched as Jason's grin changed into a broad and friendly smile he heard Jason speaking and intermittently laughing.

"Hey, doc, if you can guess what I have in my hand, you can have a bite." Jason laughed again.

"Damn, Jason, I have no idea and don't care about you coming in shouting for everyone to hear. We do not need to attract attention. Can you understand that?'

"Sorry 'bout that, doc," he apologized as he removed a something from his inside coat pocket, "brought you a special, little present. Jason proceeded to unwrap the cylindrical tube explaining to Dr. Levy, "this is a genuine, premier cannabis Bonano, my friend."

"Wrong on two counts, Jason," Dr. Levy chided Jason, "one I never smoke anything and number two, I never have, never will smoke grass --- by any name."

"That's fine by me, doc, but this rare vintage weed is manufactured in the EL Laguito Factory in Havana, Cuba. You gotta' try a hit or two."

"What is your problem today, Jason? Are you high on something? Are you suffering from an early bout with Alzheimer's or is your innate stupidity showing?"

"Well, doc, I am going to take your insulting comments as bassackwards compliments. However, --- and because, I have some really good news with an even greater opportunity to introduce you to a long-time friend of mine. He knows more about making money the easy way than either of us. At least, me."

"Jason, I don't like surprises anymore or less than Cuban cigars. In our type of business, it is vitally important that any and all communication be limited and strictly between me and you. Is that crystal clear?"

"Of course, Doc, absolutely. Can you forgive and forget this one-time slip-up --- just this once? My bud, Ted, knows nothing about our relationship. He doesn't know you and it will remain so, but he will be walking in shortly at any moment. We, three, can have a drink. I'll give him this Cuban cigar and we will limit all conversation to how the Saints are doing."

"Jason, I'm not at all happy with this situation, but to limit you from embarrassment, I will play the game."

Once again sunlight flooded into the entryway of the bar, Jason said, "Here comes Ted." and stood to greet him.

Ted looked to be well over six feet tall as he remained standing at the table. Jason stood and waited to shake hands with Ted.

Jason and Ted abruptly turned one hundred and eight degrees with their eyes locked on Corbin.

Both had flashed police shields.

Jason blurted out, "Corbin Neeley, you are under arrest."

Ted repeated the Miranda Act as Jason applied the handcuffs.

"You have the right to remain silent. Anything you say can and will be used against you in a court of law. You have the right to an attorney. If you cannot afford an attorney, one will be provided for you."

"This some kinda' funny joke --- ain't funny."

"We ain't laughing are we?" Ted flashed his badge again saying "I am with the DEA and have followed multiple incidents of interstate transportation of illicit and illegal drugs of several types."

Corbin stopped Ted's narration. "What the hell are you talking about?"

"I said Drug Enforcement Agency and Jason here whose name sure ain't Jason is with another agency you know as the Federal Bureau of Investigation. You heard of them, right?"

The FBI Agent said, "Corbin, your rap sheet looks longer than the Declaration of Independence."

"The hell with you --- whatever your name is. You son-of-a-bitch."

"Well, partner, I hope you liked being in New Orleans. If you enjoyed the Quarter, you are going to love Angola prison."

CHAPTER 44

RIDE ALONG TO ANGOLA

Corbin's decision back in Baton Rouge remained foremost in his mind. The young, court-assigned attorney is Baton Rouge had made his best efforts to make him understand that the decision of the jury was unanimous and unalterable. Corbin's memory about his plea had grown fuzzy. He could recall that he pleaded not guilty. He could not remember what he said or how or why he pleaded not guilty. The legal counsel provided to him had begged him to accept a guilty plea. Corbin failed to retain much from those conversations. Robert LeRoux, his attorney, explained that any form of a not guilty plea would result in, in all likelihood, the death penalty.

Corbin was shackled and handcuffed in a special, State Police vehicle used to transport prisoners to Louisiana State Penitentiary near St. Francisville. The 56 miles trip north up Route 61 through river bottom country and a hidden road turnoff though back woods after St. Francisville takes about one hour.

Corbin could view both sides of the roadway along Route 61 seeing only brown, swamp water. LeRoux had managed to convince two U. S. Marshalls to allow him to ride up front with them. He kept an almost continual communication with Corbin. LeRoux told Corbin that simply admitting his guilt might, just theoretically, allow a retrial for a change of plea and keep you off death row.

"Somehow, Corbin, I got to get you interested --- no, just understand that you are headed to the gas chamber. We need time to attempt to get approval to begin a change of your plea. Do you hear what I'm trying to tell you?"

"Listen to me, Bobby boy. The possibility of me taking that last, long mile to the gas chamber is slim to none. The line is too damned long." Corbin shouted through the metal, mesh barrier.

"Angola is known as the Alcatraz of the South and has the earned reputation of being the bloodiest prison in America, Corbin, you are not going on vacation or to some cushy spa."

"Bobby, count the total time you have known me. I'd say two, maybe, three weeks. If you failed to notice the M.D. following my name, I guess you just assume I am stupid."

"Stop calling me Bobby. Call me Robert or Mr. LeRoux. I am honestly attempting to help you stay alive."

"Okay, I can do that, counselor. So, tell me this before these G-men dump me off in the pen. I want to know the probability of getting a chance to change my plea." Corbin had settled down.

"Yes, I will give you my best opinion, Corbin. I cannot make you any promises. I can give you my best efforts. I do want you to consider that, at best, it is an uphill struggle. Okay?"

"--- and, Robert?" Corbin said.

"And ---you were tried for numerous crimes which I will recall for you. Not in any special arrangement, but listen to me as I run through --- not accusations, no --- guilty charges like intentional death of patients, aggravated rape of a teenager, multiple convictions of sexual intercourse without consent, forcible sodomy, pedophilia convictions, homophobic dismemberment, a long list of medical malpractice convictions, and, yes, we must not forget murder including the cremation of an FDA inspector that you had killed in what you described in court as a duel." The attorney had not included lesser crimes like pimping and pampering.

One of the U. S. Marshalls spoke for the first time. "Shut up both of you!"

The other U.S. Marshall seconded the last order. "Shut the fuck up of I'll finish you off in the car."

After the objections from both U. S. Marshalls, it took another two minutes before Corbin and Robert were again back to the awkward communication.

"Look, Corbin, I am a good attorney and I am sensitive to the needs and problems of clients, assigned or otherwise. To completely reverse the court decisions, first, it will be necessary to gain some attention. Favorable or not, that is the starting point." LeRoux said.

"Is it really worth your time and efforts, Robert?"

"Yes, Corbin, that is not the question. The better question is do you have a preference between living and dying?"

"Alright, I can tell you my exact feelings," Corbin deliberated before continuing, "of course, I would prefer to be alive. If you ask me if I deserve to stay alive even, say, in Angola's general population, yes, with no better choice, my answer is yes."

"Now, I'm hearing a slight degree of optimism. And, again, I can't make promises. Yet, there is that remote possibility of you never seeing an injection needle. Think about this, no effort equals no results."

"Tell me your opinion, Robert, if the death penalty is reversed as unconstitutional, is there light at the end of that tunnel? I mean might I, sometime in the future, see the light of day again?"

"Tough question," Robert answered, "maybe, I can give you a good opinion if the Saints will beat the St. Louis Cardinals easier."

The U. S. Marshall reached over and slapped his partner on the shoulder saying "I'm hungry. How about you?".

"Are you serious? I guess we are going to let a convicted felon headed for death row wait here with his lawyer while we eat?"

"I don't know what I was thinking. It's just that Mulligan's is up ahead in the next minute or so. That's all."

"Now, you got my juices flowing, partner. I do have an idea. We park right at the front door where we can watch out the front window. The easy way is to each take turns eating and guarding the prisoner, huh?"

"Ask the con there in the back. Ask him if he is hungry and would like to eat at Mulligan's?"

"What? Ask him if he wants to eat at Mulligan's?"

"Hell, yes, go ahead and ask him if you are that stupid."

Corbin shouted, "I don't give a shit. Go, one at a time. Maybe, one of you will choke on a hot dog. I'd enjoy that."

LeRoux stated his concern, "After you have risked jail for some food. You gonna' bring me a ham sandwich or dump me in a swamp for the alligators or some hungry crock?"

"Dump you in the swamp, lawyer!"

"And, what about your prisoner here? LeRoux asked.

"Swamp for him, too. Cops don't leave evidence."

LeRoux responded, "I appreciate your kindness, officers".

"Of course, we don't get attornies riding along. You know. One officer said.

The other officer said, "Like never. Anyway, Mr. LeRoux, we will be there in about another 20 or thirty seconds.

LeRoux responded, "Thanks for the extra time with my client, and Corbin, I will see you inside as quickly as you are processed and I get authorization and approval."

CHAPTER 45

LOUISIANA STATE PENITENTIARY (ANGOLA)

The last miles to Angola were an area of desolation through a near wilderness seemingly designed to accommodate the prisoner riders to the coming years of prison life.

The Louisiana State Penitentiary known as Angola is a maximum-security prison with some 6,300 prisoners. It is located on18,000 acres at the end of Louisiana Highway 66, around 22 miles northwest of nearby St. Francisville. Angola is bordered on three sides by the Mississippi River.

Death row for men and the state execution chamber for both sexes are located at the Angola facility.

All communication between the two U.S. Marshall, Robert LeRoux, and Corbin Neeley had ceased as the vehicle left the last paved road and continued on the lonely, dirt road approaching the prison.

Several prison guards were standing near the visiting shed awaiting the approaching vehicle. The U.S. Marshalls took command of the prisoners. Paperwork was completed and the Marshalls drove away. The Prison guards checked the handcuffs and shackles before escorting Corbin thru a private entrance.

At the bend of the Mississippi River, the Louisiana State Prison incarcerates over six-thousand inmates. About ninety of these hapless souls spend twenty- three hours each day on death row. Some of these men would be coming to their last days on earth.

Corbin E. Neeley might have been just another one of those six thousand other men in Louisiana State Penitentiary, but two things change that situation dramatically. First, he is one of some eighty - five or ninety men on death row, and secondly, he is scheduled for the gas chamber.

Upon his first arrival at Angola, he was harassed by inmates with shouts and remarks of derision. As a new arrival, Corbin took offense when anyone referred to him as 'fresh fish'. He remained standing in a single line with other new arrivals listening to instructions and demands.

Corbin pointed at the uniformed guard shouting orders and yelled, "Hey, you, officer, ah, whatever you are called, I am Dr. Corbin Neeley ---"

The frown on the guard's face could stop an on-coming train or an enraged bull. Using a large, wooden nightstick, he jammed the blunt end just under Corbin's sternum. Corbin staggered back against the wall falling to the floor. Blood kept coming from Corbin's nose as the line of convicted bumpkins froze in their positions.

As his eyes opened, he was temporarily blinded by a direct ophthalmic scope which he recognized and knew well. "Who the hell are you? First, where the hell am I?

The diagnostician scanning his eyes continued the bright light in Corbin's eye as he spoke, "Okay, you are fresh fish to me and just another big mouth patient that got in trouble right off the bat because you didn't know to keep your mouth shut as a prisoner in Angola."

"I am Corbin Neeley, physician and surgeon. So, who are you and why are you doing a retinoscopy anyway?' Corbin's pride slipped through as well as his mouth followed. Carbin grabbed at the retinoscope.

"Slow down now, bumpkin. I'm trying to help you. You were smashed by one of the Aryan Brotherhood. We got plenty of them here in this prison. The guard told me you sat down away from your own group with African-Americans. Any Aryan Nazi will kill you right at the mess table for even less than that."

"Okay, preacher, let me alone now, huh?"

"When that guard standing over against the wall says so. Why are you so eager to get out of here?"

"I want to go ahead and get into my cell is the reason." Corbin snarled.

"You are not in General Population like parolees! You won't have any cellies to keep you company. You, my doctor friend, are heading into Death Row all by yourself. In no time, doctor, you will be totally psychotic, a genuine nut case."

The guard spoke up, "Stop all the explanations and threats. He will learn soon enough. Give me the sign-out form, I'm taking him now."

The guard snapped on the handcuffs as they prepared to leave the medical room and a second guard joined them. He grabbed Corbin in a vise-like grip and jerked him along.

The guard leaned into Corbin saying, "You are allowed an hour before being shut into your Death Row cell. As a favor, this one time, we will introduce you to one of the family heads in your cell block before you go to your own cell on Death Row."

The guards pulled and tugged Corbin as he grumbled and cursed saying, "I want my own cell now."

The threesome opened several cell doors until they selected a particular one. As they shoved Corbin into the cell and locked the door, Corbin saw the Aryan monster and began pulling on the cell door to get out.

"Help, help, help me," Corbin screamed, "Guards, help me." The sound of Corbin's breaking collar bone could have been heard in any adjacent cell. Corbin's arm was twisted behind him and fingers were broken until he passed out. In the silence of that cell, the Aryan hammered Corbin's nose until it bled profusely.

The guards returned and opened the cell dragging Corbin out onto the catwalk by his heels. The guards and the Aryan nodded to each other showing prison gang signs.

Corbin seemed to be regaining some conscientiousness. The Aryan grabbed him by both ears shouting. "If I let you live. You owe me."

The guard held up his hand palm toward the Aryan telling him, "Enough, no more talk!"

CHAPTER 46

CAYMAN ISLANDS REUNION

Carleton Herrick and Max Becker met at the San Francisco airport and flew together to Miami changing planes there to fly into Havana Cuba expressly to buy some of the best cigars. Anyone who knew these two men would likely wonder why these men were going to buy expensive Cuban cigars. Either would answer that with some illogical comment. Neither Herrick nor Becker had ever smoked anything at all, much less a single cigar that can cost more than a single day's pay. The logic, if any, goes back in time to Herrick and Becker promising to visit Alex Bondurant wherever he retired. The fact is that Alex also was a nonsmoker. Still, all three felt the idea was excellent beyond question.

In Havana, Max and Carlton grabbed a cab and Max held the door for Carlton and spoke to the cab driver, "Mi amigo, necesitamos cigarros. La Casa del Habano, por favor."

"Si, senor," the driver responded, "Partaga Cigarro pronto."

Carlton turned sideways and kept his eyes on Max for the entire communication before speaking, "Hey, Max, where did that come from?"

"Necessity is the mother of invention and other stuff, Carlton. I had to use Spanish; he can't speak German, you know?"

"You never really surprise me, Max. Your Spanish sounds as real as it gets. Where did you learn to speak like that?"

"Too much time in Mexican bars, Carlton." Max smiled.

"And, can you actually speak German as well?" Carlton questioned.

"Carlton, with a Mother and Father born in Berlin, can you guess how I learned?"

As the taxi approached the cigar factory, Max and Carlton had their vision fixated on a five-story building just ahead.

"Max! Look up there at the top of the building." Carlton said.

Max read, "Partages Real Fabrica De Tabacos", and added, "and I wonder if they make these expensive cigars on every floor."

Carlton smiled and was sniffing the air. "You know, Max, with the tobacco smell this strong on the street, can you imagine what the smell will be like when we walk in?"

"Yes," Max answered, "and at Cohiba prices, the word aroma is better than the word smell."

"Of course, Max, I'd agree. Are we going to try a cigar while were here?"

"Well, Carlton, mi amigo, after flying all the way to Havana to buy cigars --- well, yes, it would be dumb not to smoke a genuinely, fresh Cohiba."

They were greeted as they entered the reception area. The greeter was an elderly man appearing to be in his sixties, or possibly his seventies. He spoke word by word haltingly. "Buenas dias, hombres. Yo estoy Jose y aqui trajando anos viente. Hablo Espanol y French." Jose extended his hand to welcome them.

"Muchas gracias, Jose. Hablas English?" Max shook his hand.

"Si --- eh, yes, I know a little English."

Carlton reached for Jose's hand saying, "Havana weather is very hot and humid. Do you have air-conditioning or something like swamp coolers here in the factory?"

"Lo siento --- sorry, but here in our factory tobacco leaves are more important than people. We can control both humidity and temperature. We do that to preserve stored inventory and guarantee the taste of our cigars.

The three men toured activities within the production areas stopping at a young woman meticulously rolling large, brown cigars. She was totally focused on her work and continued uninterrupted.

Jose said something in Spanish to the worker and she returned, "Si, si. Esplendidos. Turning away, he said,

"Bueno!"

Carlton waved his hand to Jose with a question, "What did you say to her, Jose?"

"It was only meant to be a polite interruption to her work. Her daily peso reward depends on the number of cigars that pass quality control tests." Jose explained.

"Okay," Max added, "I understand. The faster she makes cigars, the more she gets paid."

Jose squinted his eyes and moved his head left and right before talking, "Not exactly. Every cigar is different and each kind requires developed skills before assignment to the production line. What you were observing was a premier cigar called a Cohiba Esplendido. It requires the leaves of five different tobaccos and the rolling sequence of each leaf is different."

"Caramba!" Max spoke in Spanish. "Then, mi amigo, Cohiba Esplendido must be a lot of money for a smoker, right?"

"For some tobacco connoisseurs, maybe, no. You, gentlemen, will each be given an Esplendido as our gift for visiting our factory." Jose emphasized his remark by nodding his head as he spoke each word.

Max questioned Carlton, "How much do you think we would have to pay for this Cohiba back home."

"Here in our counter, a package of three Cohiba Esplendidos are available for $100 U.S.," Jose volunteered, "for you today as our guests the three pack is $88 U.S."

Jose escorted Max and Carlton to a private room used exclusively for important guests and for meetings with Cuban politicians. As they entered, the slight breeze and cool air felt like diving into a cool pool on the hottest day in Mexico City.

Jose directed the two men to the bar explaining, "Enjoy the best Rums in Cuba or whatever you would like to drink. The Daquiries are excellent and frequently preferred by many people from North America.

Carlton held up his left hand in preparation of asking a question, "Jose, are credit cards accepted in here?"

"No, sir. You are our guests here and whatever you enjoy drinking is free."

"Muchas gracias, Jose," Max said, "y el Esplendidos el mismo?"

"Lo siento mucho --- only drinks are free in here." Jose cautioned.

"No problema, amigo, I was joking." Max gave Jose a big smile.

Jose returned Max's smile and handed him a gift-wrapped package containing three Cohiba Esplandidos.

Carlton had stood silently listening to Max accept the package of Cohibas.

"Max, I am genuinely enjoying this trip with you and today has been a blast. We have choices to be made. So, we can stay in Havana tonight. In fact, we could see all the sights tomorrow or anything else that you might want to do."

"Nice to allow alternatives, Carlton. This is our vacation, our fun times, and I am not the boss. You tell me what you have in mind and we can discuss that."

"Max, I have never been a city boy and I'm really eager to get down to the

Caymans and out into the fresh air and the smell of the sea. Smoking those Cohibas together with Alex is a big thing to me, Max. Then, again, if you want to stay over tonight, that is fine too."

"Funny, Carlton, I have the same thoughts you have just voiced. I suggest we contact a travel agent and see if we can fly out tonight. Okay?"

"I'll handle it myself. I can get International Air Guide on my cell phone. Our bags have never been unpacked. In fact, they are still in the lockers where we put them at the airport.We can make a few calls and get a taxi --- I will bet we can be Grand Cayman in a matter of a few hours."

"Reminds me of Alex telling me that if he has a problem that cannot be resolved, he gives it to you. On that basis, okay, Carlton, go for it. By the way, your recommendation to keep our luggage in lockers at the airport turned out to be excellent."

With their customary cash flow, all three men could live comfortably the rest of their lives. Alex Bondurant had taken this direction intentionally with full knowledge that the three executives had planned to use market variations to manipulate the stock price of the newly structured Gigatrax. In this instance, the planning was clearly insider trading. By all appearances, the Current Ratio of Gigatrax had skyrocketed benefitting all shareholders handsomely. The increases in cash flow to Bondurant, Becker, and Herrick were better described as astronomic. To any good accountant or financial analyzer, with unparalleled growth in assets and decreases in liabilities, growth allocations should have been vested in substantial investments adding to tax sheltered liabilities. Conversely, potential assets were manipulated through creative accounting methods to grossly reward Becker, Bondurant, and Herrick with highly questionable awards.

Alex Bondurant was highly excited about meeting his friends and ex-business associates for the meeting that had been planned many years ago when they were all scrambling to meet the everyday demands or the every demand of failing their commitments and expectations of their stockholders. All these executives had made light about the interchangeability of the words executives and the word execution. Once stepping into the morass of insider trading, the daily and continuous threats of detection stress and anxiety were worst enemies. It might seem that senior executives age at far faster rates than plain, simple husbands and wives. The graying hair of American Presidents attests to this conjecture.

Max and Carlton arrive after having several martinis between Havana and Grand Cayman. Alex Bondurant had been waiting hours in advance checking the time every few minutes. Handshaking, hugs, slaps on the back, and fractured statements between the three old friends interspersed between the exchange of compliments.

Alex Bondurant's face showed wrinkling, discoloration and easily read signs of aging. Alex asked questions about Gigatrax business and then some detailed questions regarding the profit and losses of the company.

"Carlton, I knew that you spent some time in Kyoto to analyze the repeating bottom line losses."

"Yes, Alex, I sure did. I really should let Max explain the whole thing. Anyway, Alex, I finally got my comeuppance for being a half ass account."

Alex interjected, "I got to hear this, Carton. Didn't I send you to a Wharton School program for non-financial executives at on time?"

"You did," Carlton laughed, "it was limited to financial ratios and not my cup of tea."

"Sorry for getting you off track, Carlton. Go ahead with your remarks on the Kyoto story."

"Well, Alex, I'm sure that you remember the performance review you gave me years ago. I'm referring to the time you told me I make decisions like a machine gun. After what I thought was a chastisement, I was expecting a pretty low salary increase. However, I know you will recall giving me a 10% increase plus a performance bonus of $50,000 bucks."

"Oh my, I must have been drinking at lunch to make such a mistake, Carlton." Alex laughed.

"The Senior Executive at Nihon Science, Hideo Yamaguchi, picked me up at the Kyoto railway station. He knew, of course, that I was coming but, he was totally unprepared with any substantiating documentation. In fact, I must say that he was unable to answer even basic questions about Nihon Science's business plan."

Max interrupted, "Excuse me, Carlton, did it occur to you that any lack of preparation might have been due to language problems?"

"Max, I decided within the first hour with him that he must be terminated. This is what Alex here calls a machine gun decision."

"Me, too," Max nodded as he spoke, "nevertheless, your other capabilities justified the pay increase and bonus that Alex gave you. So, go ahead with Alex's questions."

"Okay, on a live conversation, you directed me to remain in Kyoto and resolve any identified problems. Max gave me instructions to consider the Japanese culture better before any major changes."

Max leaned over slapping Carlton on the knee, "At the time, I was unable to explain the master plan which Alex and I had discussed personally."

"Now, I understand that it was the most logical decision that was made. I had no idea that my success in Kyoto would result in all the cash including our Golden Parachutes."

Alex stood up extending his right hand to Carlton and his left hand to Max.

"We each cleared just slightly over $3,000,000 from the Japanese divestiture. A bit later you will be my guest in my home that was custom built for me for $1,200,000 which does not even dent my $3,00,000 from Nihon Science."

Carlton put his arm around Alex, "I have you to thank for a successful career and the good life which I am enjoying every day, Alex --- and to you too, Max, you are instrumental in my financial solvency. Thank you."

"Come on, Carlton, you are making me choke up. I think we should get on to Alex's new home and plan out the rest of our few days here in Grand Cayman."

High fives solidified the decision.

On the street, a limousine stopped for them. The driver exited the limo welcoming Alex.

"If you are ready, Mr. Bondurant?"

"What?" Carlton sounded startled, "do you know this limo driver, Alex?"

"Well, yes, I do, of course, he works for me."

CHAPTER 47

CORBIN INSULTS ARYAN BROTHERHOOD

I n these first few hours, new inmates begin an introduction to prison rules, regulations, and classification which will determine where each prisoner will be assigned. These procedures also show each prisoner will be controlled. Initially, new prisoners receive limited personal attention.

Groups of five new inmates are heavily escorted into the mess hall. The Angola mess hall like any other prison mess hall is one of the most dangerous locations in the prison. Officers assigned to mess hall duties face the danger of attack at any meal service.

Corbin and four other new prisons were herded into a mess hall by an unarmed guard. The guard instructed them to sit at a designated table which he pointed out. Corbin lagged a few steps behind his assigned group. The guard held up his hand stopping the forward movement of his group while demanding that Corbin stay with the group. The Guard stopped at one of the assigned tables explaining that the group would not be going through the food line because the food trays would be placed in front of each on them at the table.

Corbin had ventured into another area of tables occupied by inmates just beginning their meals. He eyed an empty seat, sat down and decided to ask his seat mate how to get his food tray. A large, tattooed hand grabbed him by his neck. Shocked and frightened, Corbin saw a four-leaf clover with initials in the center, AB, on the arm that was jerking him away from the table. The person now grabbing him with both hands threw him to the floor. Corbin saw a swastika tattoo on the attacker's face at the same moment two guards separated the attacker and took control of the situation.

The guard who had escorted him originally shouted at him. "Get back to your own table. Are you stupid? Sit where and when you are told. Sit with your own kind, color or religious belief!"

"Yeh, I heard you, sir. What kind of law or prison rule is that anyway? Corbin argued.

"Lucky that Aryan Brotherhood member didn't break your face for sitting with Afro-Americans."

His attacker was still standing with a guard. Corbin glanced back thinking that he might apologize to his attacker with an okay, finger and thumb signal. Corbin held up the okay signal and smiled nicely at his attacker. The Aryan Brother returned Corbin a two-handed communication with both middle fingers pointing up.

"If you want to live, you better just keep your mouth shut. Learn this or else." Corbin's guard said.

"Thanks!" Corbin muttered.

"Shut up! Are you deaf as well as stupid?"

Back at his assigned table, the man seated next to him spoke in a controlled whisper. "Listen and shut up. I have been to this rodeo more than once. I know that Nazi that gave you the double, finger salute. The Brotherhood will punish him until he kills you first."

Another one of the new prisoners at the table surveyed around the area before speaking. "This is my third rodeo in a State prison. Here in Angola, I got an all day sentence. The Aryan Brotherhood and the Mexican Mafia are all bad asses."

The guard stopped the chit chat. He pointed to four of the inmates directing," Okay, you four, get up and go through the chow line and return to the table. You other four sit here until the four return with their trays. Do not start eating until the table is full again and I give you permission to begin. Is that understood?"

All eight men and all eight trays were again positioned at the table. The guard spoke to them as he tapped his baton in tempo with his words, "Do not even touch the tray, your utensils or your food until the stick stops tapping the table.

Bam, bam, bam, bam ---- "Eat!"

One prison leaned away from the table spitting out a mouthful of whatever he had just put into his mouth. "What the hell is is this shit?"

Another prisoner answered, "Shut up and get used to it. It is government bought mystery meat. It won't taste any better next month. So, get used to it, newbie."

Two hands grabbed Corbin's tray. Corbin saw tattoos on the fingers of each hand LOVE and HATE and a dark black swastika tattoo on the forehead of another member of the Aryan Brotherhood.

"You want this, Krauthead?" Corbin said as he released the tray dumping the food on to his assailant.

The Aryan assailant grabbed Corbin by the hair pulling him away from the table.

A guard jerked Corbin's attacker away using his baton.

The Aryan stared at Corbin yelling, "You a dead man."

CHAPTER 48

CORBIN SOLITARY CONFINEMENT

Corbin's solitary confinement was a tiny cell no bigger than a regular bathroom except there was no window or any other means to see daylight, no way to feel the Sun's heat or to smell the outside air. He had been dumped into this bleak six feet by eight feet dungeon that the guard called segregation. As Corbin gained degrees of consciousness, his thoughts deepened his panic. He was beginning to realize that he would be interred in this mausoleum without contact with other people for a length of time which he did not know. The most fearful feelings were just the unknowing. These growing worries created more fears of pain and physical suffering dragging his mind into deep aggravation and sweat-wrenching panic. Nothing he could feel or see provided any sense of time. He had neither any indication of the time of day or the day of the week. He was unable to sense day from night. This sickening miasma that was eroding his mind and soul had resulted after only days, a week or more; his agony was increasing in gigantic leaps.

Whenever he could control his mind, he attempted to recoup previous days and events. He recalled the minuscule chip of quartz that had lodged into the sole of his boot. He pictured, over and over, that small bit of stone and he mentally engineered it to convert it to a sharp scalpel. Corbin had known the surgical characteristics of surgical, stainless steel, sapphire, and quality diamonds frequently used in eye surgery. Finding the quartz stone fragment embedded in the sole of his boot, stimulated his creative mind. His ability to chip away the stone and hone the edges capable of making incisions resulted in a minuscule scalpel with a cutting edge only 2 millimeters thick, 3 millimeters wide and almost 4 millimeters long. He worried that such a small piece of quartz might be very fragile. Each time he complimented himself that in his highly talented surgical hands, the danger of breakage was a minimal concern. He kept focusing his mind on his ability and increasing audacity to kill someone. Every day, he kept the blade perfectly honed using salt from his food tray. Corbin examined this quartz scalpel at every safe moment during the day. His fascination with this quartz scalpel grew into sexual arousal. Corbin spoke to this deadly, sharp, and tiny device as Medusa.

"Listen to me, Medusa," Corbin whispered as he rubbed the quartz, "I love you, dear. Do you know that?"

With utmost caution, Corbin slowly and meticulously stropped the quartz scalpel on the leather of his boot.

He mumbled and stuttered to the quartz crystal, "Medusa --- I know I caused you pain rubbing you across my boot but, I need you and love you."

Corbin alternated between bone-deep restlessness to paranoia. In depths of depression, he begged imaginary men sharing his cell to kill him. Corbin's own thoughts and personality had degraded into mental impairments, he recognized himself as Post Traumatic Stress Disorder. In more normal moments, he attempted to mentally focus on rehabilitation methods to bring his mind and body back to acceptable behavior.

Every day, he was allowed brief time, usually one hour on the catwalk for exercise. He was allowed one shower each week. He ate little of the food passed through the metal door.

Periodic fits or screaming followed by extended periods of crying had resulted in one of the guards standing and watching Corbin stretching out on the catwalk. The guard pitifully encouraged Corbin to exercise.

Corbin pleaded to the guard to allow him to get back into his cell with Medusa.

"Please, let me be alone in my room and be with my friend. I love her. I must be with her." Corbin sobbed and large, crocodile tears filled his eyes and streamed down his cheeks.

"I can do that. The handcuffs and shackles will have to go back on then. What is the name of your friend in there with you?" The guard chided Corbin.

"Her name is Medusa. Did you see how beautiful she is?' Corbin asked, "If you want to come inside and meet Medusa, it will be fine."

"Now, do you feel better back there with Medusa --- more comfortable?'" The guard spoke soothingly.

"How can you ask me how I feel? Listen to me. I have nothing to look backward to with pride and nothing to look forward to with hope. How would you feel?" Corbin whispered.

The guard walked away disregarding the question. This guard had many years of experience assigned to numerous solitary cells. He had witnessed solitary insanity in many forms. Long term solitary isolation on death row can result in insanity. To maintain his own sanity, he had learned to observe deviate behaviors as games played between the cell occupant and imaginary visitors.

The guard stepped away from Corbin's cell as another guard approached him.

"How come you keep babbling to that idiot.? He is insane and still dangerous."

"Yeh, I know that but, he is a human being and, after all, he will be dead in a matter of hours.

"No, no he is not human. He is a raving psychotic and is already dying."

CHAPTER 49

CORBIN'S LAST MEAL

orbin had refused all religious rites in preparation for his execution by lethal injection. The Warden, a devout Christian with strong Evangelical leanings sat with Corbin in his solitary confinement cell attempting to persuade Corbin to confess his sins to save himself from eternal damnation and the perpetual fires of Hell.

"Mr. Neeley, you were sentenced to death by lethal injection. You cannot change the course of events. I want you to understand that no one can save your life now. There is no possibility; none whatsoever, Mr. Neeley. You alone can still save your soul. This is a gift from God. I will allow any minister or religious leader to be allowed to sit here with you and pray for your soul. "The Warden pleaded with Corbin to take the opportunity.

"No, I will not confess whatever you are calling sins. I'm no Catholic, Warden. Sure as hell, I'm no Jew. I'm no Bible-beating, Southern Baptist. If I tell you that I am a Muslim, will you have a nice prayer rug put in my cell? No, Warden, nothing you can say will change a day in my life." Corbin's facial expression showed no fear or any emotion whatsoever.

The Warden leaned toward Corbin bowing his head and stared at Corbin's hands. "Will you pray with me, Mr. Neeley?"

"No, hell no," Corbin stammered, "God and Lucifer are no more than figments of your imagination, Warden."

"I ask you, Corbin Neeley. What if you are wrong? Only God can save your soul now."

"Warden, I got to ask you one question, okay?" Corbin scooted closer to the Warden reaching out his hand.

The Warden's hands began shaking as he spoke, "I will try to answer any question you may have."

"Sitting here in my cell, right next to me, are you frightened? Do you realize that I could kill you?" Corbin's face became an ugly sneer.

The Warden stood to exit the cell and spoke, "I do not fear you, Corbin. I will talk to you once again before you die."

The guard had been standing on the catwalk and as the Warden stood to allow him to lock the cell. He said, "Warden, sir, can I say something about this prisoner?"

"I'm listening. Go ahead. Say what you got on your mind."

"Well, sir, this man is going to be executed in a matter of hours, but he is completely unbalanced --- I mean mentally incapable of knowing the difference between right and wrong. Should we kill a man who is insane?"

"That is not a thing that can be decided here in Angola."

"Yes, sir. These Death Row assignments bother the hell outta' me."

The Warden headed back to his office.

Corbin called to get attention from the guard, "Hey, whatever you name might be --- when do I get to tell you what I want for my last meal or did Louisiana discontinue that like Texas?

"I can help you with that. The best way is for you to come up with whatever you want to eat. Then, a real chef, type guy will make anything you ask for. He has done this many times and he will cook or make anything you ask for in any way you want. And, my name is Clyde."

"Okay, Clyde, I know what I want. See if you can get the chef type guy here. I'm ready to get this nightmare over." Corbin's voice trailed off as if he was about to cry.

"I'll help you. You tell me what you want and I'll write down whatever you say and get with the kitchen, okay?"

"Sure, Clyde. Start writing! First, put this on the list. I want to start with a freshly baked loaf of sourdough bread. I want it slathered with warm, salt-free butter. Did you get that down? I want to start with two dozen, icy-cold Louisiana, fresh oysters and the gravy that goes on them --- I mean, tomato ketchup with the Worcestershire and a little Tobasco sauce. When all the oysters are gone, I want a plate of barbecued shrimp like the ones from Pascal Manales. Did you hear what I said, Clyde?"

"Yeah, I got it all wrote down here. Is that all you want? You gonna' get whatever you want." Clyde choked up a little.

"Damn near forgot the beignets sprinkled with lots of sugar," Corbin's requests were in a sing-song, "so, tell me, Clyde, when will this last feast be prepared anyway?" Corbin snickered to himself and mumbled, "the Last Feast ---- sounds weird, huh?"

Clyde turned toward Corbin's cell asking, "Huh, what did you say? I'm not supposed to be talking with you, but your strap-down is scheduled for this weekend, I think. Plenty time to get everything you want. I'm guessing your big feast will be Friday afternoon. The setup right there in your cell should be by eleven o'clock."

For days on end, Corbin soaked his right hand in the commode. It was the coldest water and the only water available. He intended to soften the skin to ease penetration of his quartz scalpel. The water might be cold enough to reduce the pain which he knew could be painful and excruciating. After extracting the tiny scalpel from the sole of his boot, he used salt that he had saved for days to clean the little blade. Corbin did know, of course, that the salt like any saline would not sterilize the quartz blade. He accepted that the salt, at least, might provide some degree of sanitation.

After soaking his hand for what he guessed was long as an hour, he studied the thumb on his right hand. Corbin could see that the epidermis was saturated and wrinkled. With concentrated care, he clamped the thumb and first finger of his left hand into a vice-like grip on the scalpel. With surgical precision, he held the sharp pointed tip just slightly under his right thumbnail. He sucked air through clenched teeth, held his breath and interrupted his actions and began rapid breathing. Finally, Corbin pulled a large breath through his nose, clamped his teeth together and forced the scalpel under the nail. He bit down on his lower lip distorting his scream. The bite to his lip squirted blood into his mouth. He tasted the blood. Blood from his thumb continued dripping on the floor. Somehow, it would have to be cleaned up leaving no trace. The pain in the thumb did not lessen. With every heartbeat, the systolic blood pressure drove the pain level to unbearable. Corbin placed his curled, right index finger under the thumb clamping the scalpel tightly. One final shove of the embedded scalpel, drove it securely affixed to his thumb. The scalpel tip extended out far enough from the tip of his fingernail to allow making an incision.

Corbin's fear and aggravation were the amounts of blood that would be seen by anyone looking at the floor of his cell. He was eager to wash the blood that was drying on his chin, throat, and shirt. Mentally, he was unable to focus on the priority of his immediate demands.

Corbin, in a moment of rational thought, considered the advantages of solitary confinement. If such an absurd situation could be imagined, it might be a total privacy to conduct activities with no audience or others interrupting your private activities. Yes, the blood on the floor could be easily seen by anyone looking into the cell except anyone looking through the slit in the door would not be able to see the floor. Corbin glanced between the blood stains on the floor and the slit in the door. The angle was much too sharp. Corbin felt confident that he had plenty of time to erase blood stains from the floor. He began using his own urine to remove stains from the floor.

The time demanded to restore his surroundings to a clean, acceptable level felt like minutes to Corbin. In measured time, over two hours had elapsed. Corbin again phased into a state of complete mental disarray.

"Medusa, I need your help," Corbin experienced the first microseconds of fear, "you can help me rearrange our cell. Wait! I hear someone coming."

Corbin only acute sense remaining was his sense of smell. As the guard opened the cell door, he breathed in the delicious aroma of all the foods atop a mobile cart that was being pushed in. His regular guard was standing inside the cell while the two guards finished setting up the array of four or five dishes and plates on top of doilies. A single rose wrapped in a paper towel was placed on the main dish. One of the guards arranged various foods on each plate. The plates were paper or plastic replicas of glass dishes. Neither guard spoke as they completed this dinner setting. Corbin had been hand cuffed and shackled the entire time the guards had been in his cell. Corbin was confused with not remembering who had put the shackles on him.

One guard spoke to Corbin. "You will be permitted to enjoy this lovely repast with the handcuffs removed. You will be allowed to remain to be alone while you eat. Guards will step outside your cell and your handcuffs will be removed through the cell door. We will remain there observing and when you are finished eating, we will escort you to the execution chamber."

The three guards did as they intended. From outside of the cell, the guard directed Corbin, "Go ahead, enjoy and when you finish, extend your hands through the door slot and the cuffs will be replaced for your last walk."

Corbin spun around like a dervish screaming like a banshee, "Not now, not today, never---". Using both hands and feet, he threw, kicked and demolished all the food and dishes including the cart.

He turned standing tall and straight as he bent his elbow bringing his right hand slightly under his right ear. As before, he clamped his right index finger against the thumb securing the quartz scalpel. He jammed the sharp point of the scalpel into the top of his carotid artery and sliced a clean incision all the way down to his collar bone.

The stunned guards were yelling at him and awkwardly fidgeting with the still locked cell door.

With every beat of Corbin's heart, the blood gushed from the artery. Losing that much blood so quickly, Corbin would bleed out quickly. He staggered as he leaned against the concrete wall. With fading strength, he incised the other carotid artery on the other side of his neck.

The guards now in the cell were shouting at each other. "Get the medic in here fast!"

"Not me. I'm going for the Warden. He ain't going to any execution now anyway."

"Damn, man, he ain't dead. We gotta' compress those bleeding arteries. We ain't executioners. I'll handle this anyway. Get the medic in here and have a guard advise the Warden. Do you see the blood still pumping from those cuts he made every time his heart beats? So, get movin' now."

Printed in the United States
By Bookmasters